The Slippery Map

The Slippery Map

by

N. E. Bode

ILLUSTRATED BY BRANDON DORMAN

HarperCollins*Publishers*

The Slippery Map

Text copyright © 2007 by Julianna Baggott

Illustrations copyright © 2007 by Brandon Dorman

All rights reserved. Printed in the United States of America.

No part of this book may be used or reproduced in any manner whatsoever without written permission except in the case of brief quotations embodied in critical articles and reviews. For information address HarperCollins Children's Books, a division of HarperCollins Publishers, 1350 Avenue of the Americas, New York, NY 10019.

www.harpercollinschildrens.com

Library of Congress Cataloging-in-Publication Data

Bode, N. E.

  The slippery map / N.E. Bode ; [illustrations by Brandon Dorman]. —1st ed.

    p.   cm.

  Summary: Oyster R. Motel, a lonely boy raised as a foundling in a Baltimore nunnery, travels through a portal to the imaginary world of his parents, where he heroically confronts the villainous Dark Mouth.

  ISBN 978-0-06-079108-7 (trade bdg.)

  ISBN 978-0-06-079109-4 (lib. bdg.)

  [1. Adventure and adventurers—Fiction. 2. Imagination—Fiction. 3. Foundlings—Fiction. 4. Parents—Fiction. 5. Convents—Fiction. 6. Baltimore (Md.)—Fiction.]

I. Dorman, Brandon, ill. II. Title.

PZ7.B63362Sl 2007   2007010900

[Fic]—dc22   CIP

                                                                      AC

Typography by Joel Tippie

1 2 3 4 5 6 7 8 9 10

First Edition

This book is dedicated to the teachers of the world, in all of their various disguises, and especially to a few glorious nuns who saved my family time and again—with noble things like art and love. To name a few: Sister Rita Estelle, Sister Jean D'Arc, and Sister John Marie—and while I'm mentioning those of a holy calling, I'd like to mention one more, Father Szupper. Oh, what brilliant, heroic souls!

CONTENTS

A LETTER FROM N. E. BODE

Dear Precious and Much-Adored Reader,

You may think that the stories of Fern and Howard (found on the pages of my books *The Anybodies* and *The Nobodies*) are the only astounding stories that I've heard in my life. Not true! Let me explain: Every person on the earth—who, at this very moment, may be pruning a bonsai tree or eating a Ho Ho or even reading a letter at the beginning of a certain book while idling in a dusty library—everyone! has an astounding story to tell.

But, you see, I'd forgotten this.

Have you ever had a day where you say to yourself, *Well, I'm a fake, a fraud. I'm not really very good at this thing I thought I was good at. I muddled my way through a bit of it, but really I'm a one-trick pony. (And I'd hoped to be at least a three- or four-trick pony!) I was just fooling myself and others. I should hang up my hat, because it's over. Done.*

Have you ever had three days in a row like that?

A month? More than a month?

Well, I have. I was in a slump. I was slumping around in my slump, slumpishly. I was, in a word, *slumpesque.* I told a few people that I was all washed up, and one told the next and the next and the next until all of these writerly writers knew.

At the lowest point of my slump, I found myself this winter at a bookish party in Baltimore where writers took turns rattling into a microphone for hours. Afterward, they came up to me, one by one, clapped me on the shoulder, and said things like, "Sorry to hear the news, Bode. Maybe you can go into some other business . . . perhaps selling cars? You could sell cars in a suit like that." And, "Well, for someone who's all washed up, you don't smell bad. I mean, I expected you to reek of failure, but you actually smell like apricots." I'd just gagged on some apricots, actually, but I didn't say anything. Instead, I slumped from insult to insult until I was outside, walking away in the snow. I was sure they were right, you see. I believe people, in general.

(You should never believe people who tell you that you aren't who you want to be! Never. They're little thieves, that's what they are!)

I just kept on walking in the snow, walking and walking, thinking, *You're no writer, Bode. You got lucky and now you're a fraud.* (It didn't help that I'd recently applied for a Fullbright award of some sort and I got a letter back stating that I wasn't even quite one-eighth bright, much less full.)

Eventually I realized that I was lost. The snow was

coming down thick, and I had no idea where I was. I saw an iron gate, and I thought to myself, *I could use a miracle right about now. A miracle would certainly help.* And that's when the gate creaked open and a round face popped out. The round face was connected to a round body. It was a nun. She looked at me. And I looked at her.

My head capped in snow, I said, "I'm surely lost."

And she waved me into a courtyard and then into a doorway. I followed her down a hall and into a kitchen. She pointed to a seat and I sat down. She handed me a cup of tea and then scribbled a note on a pad of paper. It said: *Are you an author?*

I didn't know how she knew this, of course, but I was still wearing a name tag that said: AUTHOR: N. E. BODE. She pointed to my chest. I shrugged. "I dunno. I used to be."

She scribbled again. "I have an astounding story to tell you."

I didn't really believe her, because I'd forgotten that everyone has an astounding story to tell. But stories *are* carted around in every single person's heart like—well, like what? Like an extra heart, I suppose—or, no, it's really part of the main heart. Maybe it's an under-heart, if you get me, an under-heart just for keeping stories.

And so I sat there while this nun told to me her

astounding story on small scraps of paper, one after the other torn off of a pad. The story started to take root in my imagination. (I'm a writer after all! I have a strong imagination!) The nun couldn't talk—or, could, but had promised not to. And she is the kind of grand but humble person to keep a promise.

And because I've made some promises to her, I hope I'm that kind, too.

With love, admiration, a little sloth, and gratitude,

NE Bode

N. E. Bode

CHAPTER 1
THE AWFUL MTDS
(BALTIMORE, SOUTH OF PRATT STREET)

It had been a fearful summer. Mrs. Fishback had told the nuns so. She got her news from the mini-TV that she brought with her each morning when she came to work in the nunnery kitchen.

"The Awful MTDs," Mrs. Fishback told the nuns over lunch on this one particular day. Her pudgy nose flushed with agitation, and maybe a little joy, because Mrs. Fishback was the kind of person who enjoyed a fearful summer. "Mysterious Temporary Disappearances. Kids, always kids, disappearing! Poof! Just gone! Then time passes and poof! They're back!" She explained with great relish how one girl had disappeared into her Hula Hoop. She was from the next town over and went missing for thirty minutes. Her mother was holding the hoop in her living room, weeping, with the police all around, and then the girl bounced back out of the hoop, like she'd been given a good shove.

Mrs. Fishback continued on from her perch on a kitchen stool near her mini-TV and the phone where she made all official nunnery calls, patting the fatty rump of her dog, a dachshund named Leatherbelly who had a narrow snout and labored to breathe. "Two more kids disappeared into tire swings, another into her grandmother's sofa cushions. Four minutes gone for one. Three minutes missing for another. A boy in Arbutus was gone three hours after stepping into a box that had packaged a refrigerator." She smiled brightly through the tender description of the whole town gathered around the box, keeping vigil till he was belched back into the world. "Alvin Peterly. Poor boy!" She shook her head. "And who knows what will happen today? Maybe one will disappear for good!" And then she added, with terrible glee in her voice, "Wouldn't that be awful?"

Mrs. Fishback hated children even though she had seven of them. (Or perhaps *because* she had seven of them; it's hard to say with some folks.) If she wasn't spouting off about something horrible on the news, she was complaining about her children, who were all grown now and lived far away—as did Mr. Fishback. That didn't stop her from griping that the children and Mr. Fishback had always been too messy, too loud, too costly, too rude, too runty, too slow, too feisty, too dull, too whiny, too piggish, too foul. She often said, "I should have thrown all of them out on their ears!"

She had taken the administrator job in the nunnery a few months earlier because, she assumed, there would be no children in it.

She was wrong.

This nunnery was home to thirteen nuns and one ten-year-old boy named Oyster.

As you know, ten-year-old boys aren't supposed to live in nunneries. Right now you might be saying to yourself, "Nuns are supposed to live in nunneries; that's why they're called nunneries!" Well, yes, true, but life is odd, you know, and you can't be overly rigid about the English language. (Nurses don't live in nurseries! Novels don't live in novelties! No, no. And they don't just live in novelists either; they live in hearts, you know, and everyone's got a heart.) Plus, it wasn't strange to Oyster to be living in a nunnery, even this nunnery where all of the nuns had taken vows of silence. He'd lived in a nunnery ever since he could remember, ever since he was an infant dropped off at the nunnery's gate wrapped in a Royal Motel towel and placed in a Dorsey's Pickled Foods box. This was his home.

And he was in the kitchen this very day, putting his

soup bowl in the kitchen sink, in a row of nuns who were also putting their bowls in the kitchen sink. And it should be noted that when Mrs. Fishback had said, "Maybe one will disappear for good!" she'd looked at Oyster, her eyebrows bearing down so that her eyes—a cold, vicious blue—looked hooded and shadowy in a grim way.

Mrs. Fishback had it in for him.

And at this point, Oyster didn't need anyone having it in for him. You see, the nuns had quite loved Oyster when he was a baby and when he was a cute little boy. But he was now ten, and that was a different thing altogether. He'd gotten older and antsier every year, and this summer he just couldn't stand his quiet nunnery life anymore. He wasn't able to hold himself back.

For example, when no one was in the chapel, he jumped the pews front to back like a hurdler. Once, because he could resist it no longer, he pulled the rope on the giant bell in the belfry and went riding back and forth and all around under the bell's skirt, flying, feeling like he himself was being rung and not the bell at all. Another time he'd pumped the organ—which was off-limits because it was much too loud. He simply couldn't resist it any longer. Dust spouted up from its pipes until the long notes rose in a sonorous mishmash. And he was growing a tadpole in the holy water. It was wrong, yes. But the tadpole was so happy!

The nuns, on the other hand, were not so happy. There was a complaint box drilled to the chapel wall, and the nuns filled it each week with complaints about Oyster, which were discussed in a flurry of note-scribbling at a weekly meeting that Oyster wasn't permitted to attend. He would read the notes later, however, because he was the one in charge of dumping wastebaskets, and he would sort through the notes in his room. The main thing was this: they wanted him to be more nunlike.

One had written: *Does he see* us *jumping pews, pumping organs, riding the bell cord in the belfry? No, he does not!*

There was only one nun who always stuck up for

him: Sister Mary Many Pockets, as he'd named her early on because of the many things she always had in the many pockets hidden in the long skirt of her habit—rosaries, peanuts, scissors, tape, cough drops, a tennis ball—anything, really, that you might need.

She was there in the kitchen, too, this very day. In fact, when Mrs. Fishback said that awful remark, "Maybe one will disappear for good!" Sister Mary Many Pockets patted Oyster on the shoulder, pulled a peanut from one of her pockets, cracked its shell, and looked at Oyster in a way that said, *Don't pay her any mind!*

But there was something shaky in Sister Mary Many Pockets's gaze these days. She was nervous about a revolt against Oyster, too. And so, just below the look that said, *Don't pay her any mind!* there was another look that said, *Can't you be just a little bit more like us? Just a little?*

Oyster shuffled quickly out of the kitchen, but not quickly enough to miss Mrs. Fishback saying, "It's not natural to have a boy in a nunnery, you know that. Not natural! And there's something wrong with him, don't you think? Something off about that little newt."

Oyster ran upstairs to his bedroom, knowing she was right. He had no parents, for one thing—or he had but they'd wrapped him in a Royal Motel towel, plopped him in a Dorsey's Pickled Foods box, and dumped him at a nunnery gate. Sister Mary Many Pockets was the one who'd found Oyster in the Royal Motel towel and Dorsey's Pickled Foods box, and she had kept him safe ever since. She was the one who'd named him Oyster R. Motel: Oyster because his heart was a pearl, and R. Motel for Royal Motel, because she figured it might be important for him to have these clues to his beginnings embedded into his name.

Since Oyster hadn't known how he'd gotten here, he'd assumed it was a miracle of sorts. The only birth story he really knew was of a miracle birth and so it didn't seem unusual. He was just *born*! He'd just *arrived*!

But that spring, he'd started asking questions. How exactly *did* I get here? Why *don't* I have parents? Sister Mary Many Pockets, it turns out, had been waiting for such questions, and she scribbled down the real story on slips of paper, dragging out the Dorsey Pickled Foods box and the Royal Motel towel.

Oyster tried, at first, to fit it in with the miracle. "Maybe I was born from the box! Already wrapped in a swaddling towel!" he said.

But, no, Sister Mary Many Pockets shook her head, and she wrote it out again.

Nowadays, Oyster sometimes imagined that his parents were normal parents who lived on a quiet street and that he lived with them and often played on a backyard swing set. But he had trouble with these imaginings. First of all, they made him feel guilty. These imaginings would have hurt Sister Mary Many Pockets's feelings, he was sure. But also Oyster had trouble with the logic of the imaginings. What kind of people would leave a kid in a towel in a box at a nunnery gate? What kind of people did Oyster come from? The abandoning variety. And Oyster wondered if his naughtiness this summer might just be a result of the stock he came from—the unavoidable nature of his true self.

And so Mrs. Fishback had a point that Oyster couldn't argue against, because he believed it too. There was something off about him, and even though he would try to be good—very, very good—he couldn't. The main problem was that Oyster was lonesome.

On this particular day he'd spent the morning with the only friends he had collected. Firstly, there was a sickly baby bird that he kept in his bedroom closet and fed unconsecrated hosts, worms found in deep holes he dug in the nunnery garden, and water from an eyedropper. Secondly, there was his moth collection. He'd collected most of his moths in the nunnery attic, putting them in a cardboard box with a mesh lid that he'd made himself. Lastly, he'd take time to feed the tadpole in the holy water.

Now he sat on the edge of his bed with an electric fan pointed at his head and looked out his window at the street beyond the nunnery gate—as he did every day after lunch. Oyster wasn't allowed beyond the gate. He didn't even go to school. He was educated by Sister Mary Many Pockets from mail-order textbooks. The only time he ever left was to get shots at the doctor's office.

From the window, Oyster could see the Chinese restaurant Dragon Palace, with its painted red dragon. Every day after lunch, the owner would put out a little chair, and a boy with leg braces would be plopped in the chair. He held on to a blue paper umbrella. Oyster waved to him, and the boy spun the blue paper umbrella and smiled. It was a small signal to each other that they'd developed, not having ever met.

He was the closest thing Oyster had to a real friend. But Oyster wanted more than just waving and umbrella spinning from a friendship.

Next to Dragon Palace sat Gold's Fancy Pawn Shop and Cash Store, where an old graying dog guarded the front door at night. Its greasy front window was crammed with dented silver heirlooms and old saxophones and jewelry boxes, which sometimes caught the morning sun and shone like mirrors. As its name states, it was also a cash store where people could buy money. This made no sense to Oyster.

Above Gold's Fancy Pawn Shop and Cash Store there was a billboard that read: WE BLEACH TEETH. It was Dr. Fromler's billboard: DENTISTRY FOR THE YOUNG (AND AGED). At the bottom of the sign, there was a list of Fromler's special line of MIND AND BODY PRODUCTS: BRAIN ENHANCER TABLETS, MR. PUMPED-UP MUSCLES NOSE SPRAY, CHILD-CALMING MENTHOL DROPS; PLUS: HIGH-SCHOOL-DIPLOMA-IN-A-BOTTLE KIT, FISHING AND HUNTING LICENSES, AND COUPONS FOR HAIR WEAVES.

The nuns went to Dr. Fromler when their teeth went bad. Oyster had never been to a dentist. But the billboard reminded Oyster of the outside world—and how it could have good things: enhanced brains, pumped-up muscles, calmed children, hair weaves! Oyster wasn't exactly sure what it all meant, but he loved the set of sparkling teeth on the billboard smiling down on him. At night the smile was lit with big white bulbs. The smile made him feel less lonesome.

More and more, Oyster wanted to go out there into the world, just for a quick exploration. But Sister Mary Many Pockets always reminded him of the dangers: thieves, slashers, looters, rioters, fire-eaters, evildoers, carjackers (Mrs. Fishback had taught her this term), gunslingers. The nuns had always been afraid of the outside world. For as long as he could remember, every Tuesday morning Sister Alice Self-Defense had been teaching all of the other nuns how to protect themselves in case of attack. Oyster didn't want to be thieved or slashed or looted or rioted against; and more than that, he didn't want to leave because Sister Mary Many Pockets would worry and fret and be swallowed up in sorrow (this is what she'd written to Oyster on her little slips of paper).

On this eventful day, Oyster was looking out the window when he heard a commotion downstairs: excessive screeching and much bustling. He heard more screeching and bustling down the hall of bedrooms. And there was even more screeching and bustling overhead. Screeching and bustling usually were bad news for Oyster.

This time, Sister Margaret of the Long Sighs and Withering Glare had twisted her ankle on one of his worm holes and had dragged herself into the parlor, gathering a nervous crowd along the way. At the same time, Sister Elizabeth Thick Glasses was suffering an attack of blurred vision, because Oyster had once again borrowed her eyedropper and she blindly staggered into her own locked door.

Oyster had left his moth collection in the attic by accident, and Sister Clare of the Mighty Flyswatter, on annual attic reorganization duty, had knocked over its lid. She pulled out her mighty flyswatter and waved it madly at the cloud of moths that rose, but her specialty was flies and so the moths now roamed the nunnery in a cloud.

There were so many uprisings that even the bird sitting in its nest on Oyster's desk was rattled and launched itself into the air. Oyster was overjoyed and opened his bedroom door to let it out.

Unfortunately, at exactly that moment, Mother Superior (who'd just dipped her fingers into the holy water and had been jolted by the sight of a small leaping frog—Oyster's tadpole had finally matured!) was marching to find Oyster and was charged by the bird instead. Oyster watched the flapping bird and the flapping nun, and knew that he was doomed. He ran down a set of back stairs that led to the kitchen.

The kitchen was empty except for Leatherbelly, who'd flopped on one side on the tile floor, his belly ballooning up. Oyster was a little afraid of Leatherbelly. Mrs. Fishback had taught Leatherbelly to growl at Oyster, from a smack on the nose and the command "Growl!" Leatherbelly would do his best. He'd growl, pant to catch his breath, and growl some more. Right now he just stared at Oyster with his big eyes, too lazy to growl without Mrs. Fishback around to smack his nose.

Oyster could hear a herd of footsteps: nuns. How many of them? Well, I don't know if you've ever listened to a herd of nuns before, but because of the rubber texture of the soles of their shoes, it's impossible to guess how many might be coming at you at any one time. Even Oyster, who had much experience with nuns and the sound of their shoes, was at a loss.

Shoving his shoulders to his ears, he quickly slipped into the broom closet. It was a very narrow broom closet, and broom closets are usually narrow. His head was surrounded by broom handles. The vacuum cleaner's rectangular nose blocked his feet, its one lung packed tight with dirt. The little pistols of blue cleanser bottles pointed at him. The broom closet's door, bloated from the heat, didn't shut all the way. Through the crack, Oyster watched the kitchen fill with nuns. Sister Mary Many Pockets wasn't among them. Whenever things looked bad for Oyster, he relied on Sister Mary Many Pockets to remind the nuns of how much they loved him. The first morning after Sister Mary Many Pockets had found Oyster, she'd brought him to the dining hall as if nothing was unusual. She fed him porridge. There he was, pinned to her chest like a hungry broach. And the nuns jockeyed for seats across from him, so that they could smile and gaze.

Now the nuns formed a fuming circle around Mother Superior—her wimple and veil askew from all of her flapping. (Had the bird found its way out? Oyster wondered.)

Mrs. Fishback stood next to her. She had meaty calves and a pomp of bleached hair. Leatherbelly waddled up. His belly was so big that it dragged on the ground. (The dragging of his belly had caused it to callous, which is how he'd come by his name.) Oyster could see Leatherbelly's short tail. His purplish tongue was busy licking his own shiny black nose on his thin face. He seemed to be looking at the broom closet. Would he rat out Oyster? He could. Oyster knew. He could if he wanted to.

The nuns were waiting for some kind of explanation. Oyster could hear the clicking of Sister Helen Quick Fingers's knitting needles. Mother Superior was rattled. She raised her hands to get their attention, then scribbled on a piece of paper and handed that paper to Mrs. Fishback, who read it aloud:

"Oyster is at it again, I know. But let's be calm, sisters. Let's remain steady. He's just a boy, you know." Mrs. Fishback stopped reading. She eyed the nuns and then turned to them and said, "If you ask me, a nunnery should be quiet. Imagine it here without the bother of that awful child! Imagine peace. You could have peace and live right, if you ask me. Aren't you tired of that terrible boy? He shouldn't be here! He should be sent off! It would be for his own good! It would be for *your* own good! Don't you deserve that?" She looked the nuns up and down.

Oyster could hear some of them harumphing in agreement. (The nuns couldn't talk, but they could cough, sneeze, screech, and harumph—though they used their harumph judiciously.) Other nuns, though, were shaking their heads no, no, no. He could see Sister Alice Self-Defense with her arms folded across her chest. Sister Elizabeth Thick Glasses, her eyes magnified not only by her glasses but also by deep worry. What did Sister Bertha Nervous Lips think? What about Sister Augusta of the Elaborate Belches and Sister Patricia Tough-Pork? And Sister Theresa Raised on a Farm? And Sister Elouise of the Occasional Cigarette? Couldn't he count on her? He heard Sister Margaret of the Long Sighs and Withering Glare sigh loudly and the continued anxious clicking of Sister Helen Quick Fingers, lost in a knitting frenzy.

One of the head shakers, Sister Hilda Prone to Asthma, jotted down a note and handed it to Mrs. Fishback.

Mrs. Fishback read it: "It would break Sister Mary's heart if we all decided to send Oyster away!"

Mrs. Fishback glared at Sister Hilda Prone to Asthma. She'd been beaten by kindness. Her face pruned, as if she'd swallowed castor oil and was waiting for it to take effect. Leatherbelly padded toward the closet, his nails clicking on the tile. He nudged the closet door with his squat nose.

Luckily, the mini-TV had Mrs. Fishback's attention. "Look!" she said. "The boy who disappeared!" She rushed to turn up the volume. Oyster squinted through the crack at the screen.

Alvin Peterly was a chubby boy with a big smile, his name written on the screen under his wobbly chin. He was saying, "There was a ride through the air, swinging around. Then I was in a small room with little, weird-looking people, asking me questions. There were tubs of chocolates! And they didn't want me to eat the chocolates, but I refused to answer any questions without the chocolates!"

The interviewer shook his head sadly, as if poor Alvin Peterly had lost his poor mind during his Mysterious Temporary Disappearance. "There you have it," he said wearily. "Reporting live from Arbutus."

Leatherbelly whined at the door and scratched it twice. Mrs. Fishback snatched him up, petting him fiercely. "If only Oyster R. Motel would disappear! Imagine! It would be beyond our control. Nobody's fault. Poof! All of our troubles would be gone!"

There was a silent heated moment. Were they all contemplating it? Oyster gone? They all seemed poised on this one moment. Oyster wanted to speak up for himself: *Remember you once loved me? Remember?* Oyster had been a miracle, really. He was born from a Dorsey's Pickled Foods box, already wrapped in a Royal Motel towel, born right at the nunnery's gate, a miracle just for the nuns. A miracle!

But it was clear that the nuns were no longer swayed by the miracle of Oyster R. Motel. They weren't remembering how much they'd once loved him. It was clear that they were imagining peace. A world without the bother of awful Oyster up to no good. And from the depth of the silence, Oyster could only imagine that they were deciding that they liked the idea. And it made him feel so sad that he felt sick.

Just then Sister Mary Many Pockets flew into the room. She was nervously cracking peanut shells, leaving a small trail of them in her wake. She looked under the table and raised her hands in flustered panic. Oyster knew that she was looking for him. He wished she wouldn't! He was trying to be invisible, especially right now when the dust in the broom closet was getting to his nose. He had to sneeze. And, worse, Leatherbelly had wrenched his head out of Mrs. Fishback's arms, and he was growling in the direction of the broom closet.

"What do you want?" asked Mrs. Fishback.

Sister Mary Money Pockets put out her hand, indicating Oyster's height, indicating Oyster himself.

Mother Superior shrugged. The other nuns glanced around the room guiltily. And Leatherbelly let out a knowing bark, but no one paid him any attention.

"Maybe he's disappeared!" said Mrs. Fishback, an insincere panic in her voice.

Mother Superior pointed at the television. And there the broadcaster was, recapping the Awful MTDs.

Sister Mary Many Pockets's eyes grew wide. She popped some peanuts and shook her head.

And Oyster was thinking, *Maybe it* would be *a good thing to disappear.* Alvin Peterly and the girl lost in the Hula Hoop and the kids who went missing in the tire swing—well, maybe they were lucky. Maybe they didn't want to be where they were because maybe they weren't wanted. Oyster thought, *If I disappeared, I'd want to stay gone. And the nuns would regret that they ever wanted me to disappear.*

He suddenly felt a thick sadness in his throat. He turned away from the cracked door and the broom handles and the vacuum crowding in, the detergent pistols all aimed at his face.

He leaned against the back of the broom closet. And then the wall gave.

It opened to breezy, cool dark air, and Oyster had to lurch forward to keep from falling. One of the brooms that had been propped against the wall, the only broom with a green handle, immediately fell out into open air, endlessly spiraling.

Oyster felt hard metal hit the backs of his legs. It disappeared and struck again, but this time he grabbed the curved edge of something made of polished metal. He started to slip again. He pushed the metal object away, but soon it was back, banging the backs of his knees, causing them to buckle. The curved metal edge now seemed more like the mouth of a large bucket. He felt like he was falling into the bucket, like it was trying to scoop him up against his will. He tilted back farther into the now seemingly endless broom closet toward the gusty air. He tried clawing his way back. His feet kicked out from beneath him as the bucket kept riding up. Finally he threw himself forward and kicked open the closet door. Brooms fell to the floor in a clatter, and while the rest of him was still being pulled into the gusty darkness, Oyster grabbed on to one broom, locked lengthwise across the broom closet's door frame.

All of the nuns turned to the closet and gawked at him. Leatherbelly looked up with his popping eyes. Cold, breezy air billowed into the kitchen. Oyster held on to the broom tightly. It was the only thing keeping him from being carried off by what he could now see by glancing over his shoulder was, in fact, a large silver bucket with fancy molding.

Mrs. Fishback squeezed Leatherbelly to her chest, hugging him so tightly his eyes bulged even more than normal. "It's that rotten boy!"

Mother Superior gasped, her veil lifting in the chilly wind.

Oyster stared at Sister Mary Many Pockets. "It's going to take me!" he shouted, the windy dark whipping around his head, the bucket trying to scoop him up.

Sister Mary Many Pockets ran to him. She grabbed the broom with one hand. With the other hand, she pulled a long bundle of rope from one of her many pockets.

Sister Hilda Prone to Asthma grabbed the rope and tied it around Oyster's waist. The other nuns picked up the rope and started pulling—a tug-of-war with the wind and the grasping bucket—Mother Superior as the anchor. They heaved all of their weight backward, squatting, the way they did when they had to ring the big bell in the belfry.

The wind was strong, but the nuns were stronger. Oyster was inching forward, away from the blackness at the back of the broom closet. Sister Mary Many Pockets held tight, and soon Oyster couldn't feel the bucket at all. Suddenly the back of the broom closet was there. His feet knocked against it, the gusty air stopped, and

Oyster came tumbling out, landing in a heap of nuns, banging his tooth against the tile floor.

Mrs. Fishback let out a huffy breath and glared at Sister Mary Many Pockets and Oyster. "Well, aren't you lucky, Oyster." She swatted Leatherbelly's nose, and he growled and panted and growled.

Oyster said, "I didn't mean to. I wasn't trying to cause trouble." He turned to all of the nuns. "Remember when I was a baby? Remember?" And then Oyster finally let out his sneeze.

Into the silence Mrs. Fishback said, "You've wrecked a tooth, stupid boy!"

He ran the tip of his tongue over a new chip in his front tooth. He'd have to go to the dentist, wouldn't he? Out into the world! The thought made him smile.

Mother Superior sighed.

Sister Mary Many Pockets looked at Oyster and his chipped tooth. Oyster looked at her flushed face cupped by its wimple. She pulled a few peanuts from one of her many pockets and mouthed his name, *Oyster R. Motel.* Then she shook her head, and Oyster could feel her saying, *You scared me, Oyster.* Sometimes it was like this; her heart could speak to his. She pulled a tissue from one of her pockets. She closed her wet eyes and pressed them.

Then there was a flurry of motion in the air over

their heads. Sister Mary Many Pockets, Oyster, Mother Superior, Mrs. Fishback, all of the nuns, and Leatherbelly, too, looked up to see a flock of moths led by a scrawny bird skitter and bump through the kitchen—in one door and out through another.

CHAPTER 2
AN UNSLIPPERY MAP OF LITTLE USE

Oyster sat in the passenger seat of the nunnery van so that, as Mrs. Fishback put it, she "could keep an eye on him." The problem was that Oyster wasn't very tall, and his seat belt, batted by the wind through the open window, was either flapping around his face or choking him. It didn't help matters that Mrs. Fishback drove madly while applying a thick coat of lipstick, circling her mouth. She didn't wear a seat belt at all. She careened over lanes, hollering at the other drivers. Leatherbelly dug his nails into her white polyester pants, his rump with its narrow tail skidding first one way and then the other over the vinyl seat.

As Mrs. Fishback bullied her way across town, she talked about Leatherbelly's own appointment to have his teeth looked at by the dentist—on the cheap, a two-for-one special. "He's the one who needs dental work!

Look at my little prince. His poor, little, crooked smile. Who cares if Oyster R. Motel has a chipped tooth? Leatherbelly is the one who brings great joy into the world, aren't you, baby?"

Oyster ignored her as best as he could. He was trying to concentrate on the view. He only got these little wisps of the real world once or twice a year, and it didn't seem fair that the seat belt was in the way. He was only getting to see bits, little snapshots. The trucks let out exhaust clouds, tipping the caps from their tall pipes, like music from the chapel organ. Ships moaned in the harbor, where he saw bits of the paddleboats and the bright, looming Domino Sugar sign. Buses barreled and then stopped and then barreled again. Oyster was wide-eyed, drinking it all in as fast as he could.

Oyster was most disappointed that he didn't see any children. It was the rampant fear of the Awful MTDs. The All-Talk All-the-Time AM station's announcer on Mrs. Fishback's radio was reporting closings due to the Awful MTDs: Bible camps, Girl Scout outings, Camp Waterloo, Camp Ipshanooka, all closed. Day-care centers too: Shining Star, Tiny Tots. Sports were canceled due to a girl's disappearance into a soccer goal. And because a boy had slipped into the top of a tunnel slide at a public pool and hadn't come out the bottom for two hours, public pools were shut down too.

Since the incident in the broom closet, Oyster was now fearful of the Awful MTDs too. He'd woken up feeling strange and still did: buzzy in his limbs, a little stunned. His mind kept replaying the gusty air, the darkness, the metal bucket trying to scoop him up and take him away. When he closed his eyes, sometimes he saw the chubby face of Alvin Peterly talking to the reporter about the ride through the darkness and the little room of odd people and the tubs of chocolates. Was it true? Sister Mary Many Pockets was so afraid of losing Oyster that she'd wanted to come to the dentist to hold his hand. But Mother Superior had put her on candle-snuffing duty after morning prayers.

Oyster knew the nuns were all a-dither about the incident in the broom closet. They all seemed to be shaking their heads, their brows knotted up, their breaths huffy. *What to do?* they seemed to be saying to themselves, to one another. *What to do?*

And what *would* they do? Oyster wanted to know. Would they send him off? *Probably,* Oyster thought. It was too much, wasn't it? Too much to have a boy in the house, especially one who caused so very much trouble.

Oyster's mind was going in every different direction. He was jangled. The world was bigger than it had been the day before. He'd always wanted to get out and see it, but now the world didn't begin or end just where he thought it had. (Even ordinary broom closets didn't begin or end just where he thought they had.)

And so it was harder to believe that he was born from a Dorsey's Pickled Foods box at the nunnery gate. Well, he had known that all along, hadn't he? He'd had parents. Of course he'd had parents. No one is really born from a box. His parents still existed in Oyster's imagination, even though they were fuzzy. *Some*one had wrapped him in the towel and put him there and carried him to the nunnery gate. But the thing that was hardest for Oyster to contemplate was the question *Why?* He didn't like the answers he came up with, so he tried hard not to think of that question.

He should be counting his blessings. He thought of Sister Mary Many Pockets who, at that very moment, would be balanced on a pew, holding the snuffer on its long stick, placing its metal cap over the flames one by one. He was lucky, really, wasn't he? He could have been left across the street and fed to the mean dog that guarded the Gold's Fancy Pawn Shop and Cash Store.

One of the van's tires slammed into a deep pothole and then bounced back up again. Mrs. Fishback ignored it. "Well, Dr. Fromler can't be very good if he's hidden his office!"

"Hidden it?" Oyster said.

"Well, it isn't where it's supposed to be!" Mrs.

Fishback screeched at him, her lips a terrifying red.

"Are you lost?"

"Don't be an idiot, boy; of course I'm not lost! Get out the map!" She pointed at the glove compartment.

Oyster popped it open. Inside he found a folded map, worn at its edges. Because the title of this book is *The Slippery Map*, you may be looking for an unusual map to appear, a slippery map, a highly unusual, maybe even magical map! (Even though right now you don't know how magical a slippery map is.) But this map stuffed into Mrs. Fishback's glove compartment was a very ordinary map. Oyster tried to spread out the map on his legs, but the map was flipping around in the breeze coming in through the windows. Finally it was swept out of his hands. It slapped onto Mrs. Fishback's face, where it stuck for a moment. She swiped it away and it whipped out the window.

Mrs. Fishback's eyes narrowed to angry slits. She cinched her lips tightly. "Oyster! You numbskull!"

Now, the map may have been a very ordinary map, but the glove compartment was not, at this moment, an ordinary glove compartment at all.

Oyster realized that the wind had grown stronger and, worse, colder, shooting out of the glove compartment, which was still hanging open. It was the Awful MTDs, returned. He reached to shut the glove compartment, but the wind was full strength now, jet stream–like. There was no closing the little door.

"Oyster!" Mrs. Fishback was screaming now. "Oyster, make it stop!" She was zigzagging all over the road. The wind pressed Leatherbelly against the seat. His cheeks opened and flapped like sails, revealing his pink-and-black gums.

Oyster leaned over to the gusting glove compartment. He stared inside. "Hello?" he shouted. "Please stop!"

He listened to the rushing air and then he thought he heard a rustling of voices.

"What did he say?" one was asking.

"Is it him?" he heard another voice ask.

"It can't be! Not possible. They can't call on us, can they? Unless . . . it *is* him!"

"Listen! Hush!"

"How can I hear with you talking all the time, Ringet?"

Oyster had never heard of the name Ringet. He leaned in again, the cold air rushing into his mouth, and shouted more loudly. "Hello? Who are you?"

"Push it in the bucket! Send it back!" Oyster heard someone shouting.

He thought they might be talking to him. "Push what?" he called back.

"Do whatever they say!" Mrs. Fishback cried. "Give them whatever they want!"

Oyster squinted into the hole. He saw something glint. The silver bucket, gliding toward him. And there was something in it. Something bristled and fierce looking. Oyster reared back from the glove compartment, the wind whipping around his head.

"What is it?" Mrs. Fishback cried. "What is it?"

Leatherbelly whined and pawed at Mrs. Fishback, who was trying to keep her hands on the wheel.

"I don't know!" Oyster told her.

The bristly muzzle poked its way through the glove compartment and shot toward Oyster's face. Did it have teeth? Oyster dodged and saw its stiff, snakelike body fly by. It landed behind Oyster, on the floor between the backseats. Mrs. Fishback finally wheeled crazily into a parking lot, swerved into a spot, and slammed on the emergency brake. Since she wasn't wearing a seat belt, her pudgy nose smacked the steering wheel; and she screamed out, covering her face with her hands.

The wind became a high-pitched whistle, like a kettle—as if a hole inside of the glove compartment were closing to the size of a straw—and then the gusty wind disappeared altogether. The air was still. The glove compartment was a glove compartment again. Oyster slammed it shut, but he was too afraid to turn around.

"Oyster R. Motel!" Mrs. Fishback whispered hoarsely. "You fix this. Hear me? You'd better fix this." Leatherbelly had landed in the footwell. He peered up nervously. Mrs. Fishback pulled her hands from her face. Her nose was bleeding. The blood was on her hands. "I could bleed to death!" she said, tipping back her head and pinching her nose. "And it would be your fault!" She grabbed Leatherbelly and got out of the car. "You go back there, Oyster, and find out what it is! Find out what is back there before it attacks me!"

Oyster had no choice. He unbuckled his seat belt and climbed to the back of the van. He saw the spiky face, but the rest was hidden under the seats. "It's okay," he said to himself. "It's going to be okay." He slowly squatted.

As it turns out, it didn't have a muzzle or a stiff snake body. It was the green-handled broom, returned. Oyster stared at the broom. He nudged it with his foot.

"What is it, Oyster R. Motel, you evil boy? What?" Mrs. Fishback yelled from outside the van.

"A broom. It's our broom, I think. One of our nunnery brooms."

"How terrible. A nunnery broom, one of our own, turning on us!"

He knelt behind the seats, out of Mrs. Fishback's view, and examined it. How strange, he thought, that they (whoever they were) had returned it. It seemed like they were looking for someone in particular. But who? Not him. Not even the nuns in the nunnery wanted him anymore.

The tip of the broom handle had a caked-on splotch of something pink. Oyster picked off a chunk of the pink stuff. He sniffed and it smelled nice, like candy. Against everything the sisters had taught him, Oyster decided to nibble off just a tiny bit.

It was the sweetest thing he'd ever tasted. Pink chocolate.

CHAPTER 3
THE MAPKEEPER

Mrs. Fishback's bloody nose was fat and bruised. She was pale. In a dramatic, woozy voice, she said, "Get help, Oyster! We're lost and I'm going to die! Go, run! Get help! A doctor! Find a doctor!"

Of course, Oyster knew that Mrs. Fishback was not going to die. She only had a bloody nose. Oyster had gotten one once when he'd whacked his nose on the back of a pew after slipping on some frankincense (or had it been myrrh?) that had leaked out of a canister in the chapel. It was really no big deal.

Regardless, Oyster took one final look at the broom, and, with the sweet taste of pink chocolate still lingering in his mouth, he got out of the van and headed up the street. It wasn't a very busy street. The shop windows rattled with air-conditioning units that leaked onto the sidewalk. The heat was steaming off of the pavement. Oyster wasn't sure where to find a doctor on a street like this—Artie's Arcade? It was closed due to the Awful MTDs. Bristol Bank? He cupped his hand to the window and looked at a maze of red velvet rope leading to a counter and a pale woman on the other side fiddling with her nameplate: MRS. FLORNT. She didn't seem as if she'd be very good at consoling the hysterical Mrs. Fishback. No, she seemed to lack the necessary *mustard*—as Mrs. Fishback had once said of Oyster—and zip. She lacked zippy mustard, Oyster decided. He moved on.

The next shop had no sign, only a plate-glass front with a small placard that read: MOVING. CLOSED. When Oyster looked in through the window, he saw boxes, and rows of shelves filled with rolled-up scrolls of some sort. A small figure shifted at the end of one of the rows. There was a dusty importance about the shop that he couldn't explain, a mysteriousness. He walked to the door and tapped on the glass. He wasn't sure what he was going to say. He'd nearly forgotten about Mrs. Fishback. He just wanted to go inside. It dawned on him that he'd been wanting to be out in the world, and here he was, happening upon a mystery.

The figure stopped, looked up. It was a woman with a trimmed head of gray hair and a sharp face, pinched eyes, and pinched lips—as if she'd bought them in a matching set. She put her hands on her hips and stared; and then, as if recognizing Oyster, she waved him in.

Oyster pushed open the door. Bells jangled from the inside handle. The room held a small puff of coolness, just a small puff, from a hardworking air conditioner thrumming out of view. There was a back room with a door standing open, revealing a bit of an office desk and a chair on wheels. The dust motes churned slowly. There were scrolls of varying sizes stuck in cubbies. Some were fat and long, others short and thin. The labels on the cubbies were the names of people: GULOTH GLUTEN, DONALD OSTERMANN, LOLA HEFFERNAN, THE BAGGOTT TWINS, ALEXIS MAXWELL. And the labels on the cubbies matched small metal labels nailed into the wooden poles of the scrolls. There was one cubby in particular that caught Oyster's eye. It had two names: EDDY WARBLER and FRANCINE MIGHT. But there was no scroll. Instead, there was only a little slip of folded paper that read: *STOLEN*, in red handwritten letters.

"Yes, yes, what is it?" the woman said. She had the oldest, most wizened face that Oyster had ever seen—and Oyster, keep in mind, had been raised among old wizened faces in a nunnery. She wore a large metal name tag that read: CARTOGRAPHER AND KEEPER. It was so large, this name tag, and she was so frail, that it weighed her down, tipping her forward. The extra skin that sagged below her chin swayed forward. Her skin was leathery like the scrolls that protruded from their cubbies.

"Um, well, I . . ." Oyster couldn't remember why he was there. He wanted to know what the scrolls were, especially the one marked *STOLEN*. But there was a reason he was there besides that, wasn't there? He stammered on a bit.

"What is it? I don't have all day! I'm busy here, moving again. Maps into boxes. So that I can get to the next spot and take maps out of boxes. Much to do!" She started rummaging through a box at her feet.

"Maps?" Oyster asked. "Is that what these are?"

"Yes," the woman said, "of course!"

He walked up to one of the shelves, reading the names: FRANCESCA HAROLD, ALLEN BLOOM, MICHITRA HUNAN. he walked closer to the one marked *STOLEN*: EDDY WARBLER and FRANCINE MIGHT. "What are they maps of?" Oyster asked.

The woman paused, frozen mid-slouch. She stared at Oyster, eyeing him up and down, and then she asked, "How old are you?"

"Ten," Oyster said.

"Name, please!"

"Oyster R. Motel," Oyster said.

She disappeared for a moment and then reappeared with an oxygen mask strapped to her face and pulling an oxygen tank on wheels behind her. It rattled like a tea cart. She walked to her office, opening a massive book on her desk, bigger than the Baltimore phone book. She whipped through some pages and stopped. "Yes, yes," she said, her voice muffled by the oxygen mask. She walked toward Oyster. "You haven't given up on it. Not yet! But they usually all do in time."

"Give up on what?" Oyster asked.

"Your IOW," the woman said.

"IOW?" Oyster asked.

The woman sighed with irritation. "Imagined Other World. We all have them as children. I'm the Mapkeeper of all Imagined Other Worlds, a cartographer by trade. I map the Imagined Other Worlds of children, or at least I get them started. They usually become self-propelling."

Oyster looked at her, bewildered.

"Once I get them going, they start to record the child's imaginary updates on their own."

Oyster was still bewildered.

She forged on. "And then I keep the maps. If I don't, who will? People outgrow imaginations, you know, most often when they become adults. But I keep the IOWs, just in case."

In case of what? he wondered. He turned a small circle,

gazing up and down the row of cubbies. "All of these are Imagined Other Worlds! Wow! There sure are a lot." It was such a strange thing, he almost couldn't believe it was true. He wanted to tell the Mapkeeper that he'd just been a part of something strange himself—the silver bucket trying to haul him off into a windy darkness, the disappearance and return of the nunnery broom. It seemed like the world was offering up an abundance of strangeness, and that this Mapkeeper was accustomed to such things. Maybe she could explain some of them to him. He thought of the name that he'd heard through the glove compartment: Ringet. He thought of Eddy Warbler and Francine Might's stolen map.

His eyes landed on the empty cubby again. "What happened to that one?"

The Mapkeeper pushed her oxygen cart up to the empty cubby and stared at it. She pulled the oxygen mask up to the top of her head. She gave a smile—but it was a stern smile, the kind you give to a worthy opponent. She touched the label. "It was a joint possession. Two children had created an IOW together. A boy and a girl: Warbler and Might. Many years ago, they happened upon me and my collection. They stole their map and slipped inside it."

There was something about this last sentence that made Oyster's heart pound loudly in his chest. It was as if he was hearing something that he was meant to hear, as if his whole life had been ticking toward this one sentence: "They stole their map and slipped inside it."

"They did *what*?" Oyster asked quietly.

"The maps are slippery," she explained, peering at him over her glasses. "One can slip inside of a slippery map, if it's large and well imagined. One can slip into the World itself. All you need is the sharp edge of something and, well, it's best to travel through the Gulf of Wind and Darkness *in* something."

"Really?" Oyster said. He didn't know what the Mapkeeper was talking about. Not really. Yet he loved the idea of slipping into a map—into his own map. "Did those two kids ever come back?"

"No," the Mapkeeper said. "They've remained. They were needed, it seems, inside of their map. The Other Worlds exist, you know. Fully and completely. And those two, well, they were do-gooders; and now they're grown-up. And, at the moment, quite stuck."

"Stuck?"

The Mapkeeper flipped her hands in the air. "Well, it was their own fault!"

Oyster understood the boy and girl wanting to stay. He understood wanting to be needed. If only the nuns needed him, well, then he'd have a place

among them. He wouldn't be just a nuisance anymore. He wanted to know whether he had a map. His
name was in the book. Was his Imagined Other World
here somewhere? Was it possible? He wanted to ask
but didn't want to sound forward, and so he spoke
like he was just musing aloud. "I wonder if you have
one for Mrs. Fishback? She was a child once. And for
Sister Mary Many Pockets? For me? You don't have
one for me, I bet."

"Why do you say that? Have you imagined another
World?"

He *had* imagined another world: a green backyard
with a swing set and his parents and the boy from the
Chinese restaurant—but he couldn't help but get interrupted by the thought of Mrs. Fishback with her
bloody nose, probably cursing him this very moment
for being a numbskull.

"I'm a numbskull," Oyster said. "I'm difficult. I'm too
much trouble."

"You are?"

"Yes."

"Who says so?"

"The nuns and Mrs. Fishback. They'd rather I
weren't around."

"The nuns and Mrs. Fishback? What about your
parents?"

"I don't have any."

"Right, right, of course," the Mapkeeper said, as if she'd just been stupid for asking the question. "Did this Mrs. Fishback and the nuns all say that you're trouble?"

"Not out loud," Oyster said. "I mean, the nuns can't talk. But they feel it. I know they do."

"Oh," the Mapkeeper said. "And what do you think?"

"I want to escape." Oyster was shocked that he'd said this aloud. He'd thought it, of course, but he was surprised to hear the words bounce around the shop. "I want to go and be a hero, and prove to them that I'm worthy."

"Worthy of what?"

"I don't know," Oyster said. Honestly, he didn't.

The Mapkeeper started to shuffle down the row, dragging her oxygen cart, her eyes scanning the labels. "Well, it so happens that if your name is in the book—and your name *is* in the book—then your map is here." Oyster followed her closely, his ears pounding.

"Oyster R. Motel. Oyster R. Motel." She stopped. Oyster nearly bumped into the oxygen cart.

"Here it is." She pulled over a nearby step stool and climbed to a shelf so high that Oyster couldn't see what was up there. His view was blocked by some mammoth scrolls sticking out here and there overhead. Some of them were so big that Oyster thought if they fell, they'd

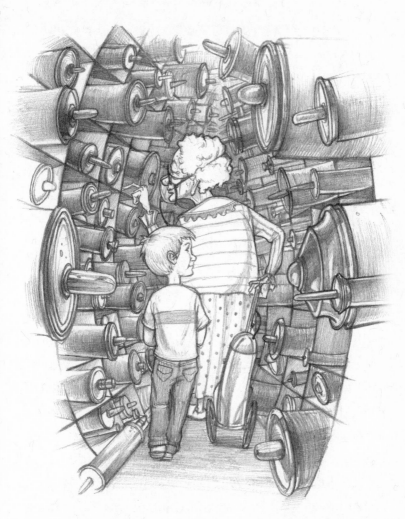

most likely smash his head. The Mapkeeper was reaching in, up to her elbow, and patting around. Was his cubby empty? Maybe so. Probably so. Who would keep track of his Imagined Other World? Not worth the time, most likely.

But then the Mapkeeper said, "Aha!" And she pulled out something small and tight, the size of a pack of Life Savers.

"Oh," Oyster said. "Is that all?"

"Yes," she said. "I'm afraid so. Haven't done much imagining about your Other World, have you?"

Oyster shook his head.

"And how did you chip that tooth?"

Oyster ran his tongue over the tooth. "I fell down on my face. And I got in trouble too."

There was a quiet moment. Oyster felt awful. He could feel the moment swelling with misery. His map was so puny, so sad, really.

"Look here, Oyster R. Motel," the Mapkeeper said. "You should learn to have a little more faith in yourself. You've got a great imagination. You just haven't unleashed it."

Oyster nodded. He couldn't look at the Mapkeeper, but he could feel her looking at him, regarding him very seriously.

"People think they want this thing or that. Sometimes they just want and want and want. They can become lousy and rotten from wanting. But truly, once you find out what you really, really want, Oyster, you'll learn that you've already got it. Do you understand?"

"Not really," Oyster said.

Then the Mapkeeper leaned in close to Oyster's face. She said, "I have three rules."

"You do?" Oyster looked up into the Mapkeeper's pruned face, into her keen, narrow eyes.

"Do you want to hear them?"

"Yes!"

"First, look at people and try to find the truth within them. You need to understand people, really understand them, if you're going to be a hero, Oyster. Do you follow?"

He nodded. He wasn't sure that he followed, but he was trying.

"Second, beware of things that shine and glitter and make promises, especially promises that play on your weaknesses. Do you have weaknesses?"

"Yes," Oyster said. "I've got plenty."

"Beware, then," the Mapkeeper said. "Third, you have to have a strong imagination."

"Oh," Oyster said.

"I know you don't have a strong one now, but you have to be willing to work on your imagination so that you can *become* something."

"I guess so," Oyster said. He felt defeated already.

"Well," the Mapkeeper said. "Do you want to see your map?"

"I guess," Oyster said.

"Okay, then, quickly," she said. "I have work to do." She handed it to Oyster.

It fit nicely in his hand. He opened it quickly. There it was: a colored map of a yard, a house, a swing set. It was small and lacked detail—it was just a crayon square with a labeled *X* for the swing set.

"Do you recognize it?"

"Yes," Oyster said. "I do." Oyster felt hungry for it. He wanted to have the map, to keep it. He wondered if it would satisfy him—just to have the map, to carry it around in his pocket.

The phone rang at that moment, a loud jangle from the office. It startled Oyster. He dropped his map. It hit the ground and curled up like a pill bug and rolled under the shelves.

"I've got to get that phone," the Mapkeeper said. "Collectors! Always after their piece of the pie!" She started down the row, then looked back at Oyster. "Reach under there and get that map," she said. "I can't bend so well anymore. Leave it on the counter, and I'll put it up later."

Oyster did. He reached down and pulled out his puny map. He looked at the Mapkeeper sitting in her office chair talking to someone in a heated way.

And this is the moment when he realized that he was going to steal the map, of course. It had been done before—like the boy and girl had stolen theirs those many years ago. *It's my map,* Oyster thought. *It's my map, after all, not hers. You can't steal what already belongs to you.*

So he turned, put the map in his pocket, and walked quickly to the door. The bells—he'd forgotten—jingled loudly.

The Mapkeeper yelled out, "What's that now?"

Oyster stood in the open doorway. He looked back at her. She was standing in her office, staring at Oyster down one of the rows. Her hand was cupped over the phone's mouthpiece.

"I've got to go!" Oyster said. "I forgot that there's an emergency! Someone with a bloody nose who needs a doctor!" And then, without waiting for her answer, he stepped out onto the sidewalk, letting the door shut, and took off running back past the bank with its velvet ropes. He rounded the edge of Artie's Arcade.

And there was the nunnery van and Leatherbelly and Mrs. Fishback with a plug of tissue stuffed up each of her nostrils.

She saw Oyster and scowled viciously. "You left me here!" she said. Oyster had never seen Mrs. Fishback so afraid—not even earlier when she'd thought they were being attacked in the van by the broom. "Why would you do that?"

"You told me to get help!" Oyster said.

"I don't like being left," said Mrs. Fishback, her voice shaking. She lifted Leatherbelly and nuzzled him under her chin. "*You* would never do that! You love me!"

Oyster remembered what the Mapkeeper had said—that some people had gone rotten with wanting. Mrs. Fishback wanted to be loved, not abandoned, but that just made her miserable to be around. Oyster could see it clearly now. He had to learn to understand people. Maybe he could do that. Maybe.

"You're just lucky I'm not dead! But we're still lost! How is Leatherbelly going to get his teeth cleaned and possibly get braces now? How, I ask you? This is all your fault!"

Oyster shook his head. "No, we aren't lost," he said.

Because from his view here, looking back, he saw a sign in the sky above a building at the back of the parking lot. Dr. Fromler's sign. They'd made it after all! Dr. Fromler! The famous Dr. Fromler who was all-good, all-loving, all-glittery smile—he'd shined his glittery love down on Oyster for all of his life. Oyster would have recognized those glowing teeth anywhere.

Standing there in the bright sun, staring at the nunnery van and Mrs. Fishback with the tissues up her nose, he wondered what he would do with his stolen map. If he imagined his green yard and his house and his swing set and his parents and the boy with the blue umbrella clearly enough, with more detail, would the map become big enough for him to slip into that Other World? Maybe if he imagined more rigorously, his map would grow and he could meet his parents on the other side, by the swing set, with his friend from the Dragon Palace.

Oyster felt strong, almost hopeful. He pointed up at the sign, the giant, glittery teeth smiling down on them. "We're here," he said.

CHAPTER 4

DR. FROMLER'S DENTISTRY
FOR THE YOUNG (AND AGED)

The walls of Dr. Fromler's waiting room were striped red and white like a circus tent. Instead of chairs, there were merry-go-round horses. Oyster had never been to a circus or seen a merry-go-round, except in books. He'd never really had much in the way of toys. So Oyster liked the first horse he saw, a bright blue horse with giant white teeth. All of the horses had giant white teeth. There were pictures of clowns and cowboys and train conductors all with giant white teeth. There were puzzles of teeth, and helium SMILE balloons on strings, bobbing overhead. Oyster wanted to sit on the merry-go-round horse, but he knew Mrs. Fishback would yell at him, so he just petted the horse's ears with one hand. The other was in his pocket. He was holding on to his map, not willing to let go of it for a moment.

"Stop it!" Mrs. Fishback said. "This is a dentist's office, not a petting zoo!"

The only things that resembled ones in regular offices were the small coffee tables—adults can't have a waiting room without coffee tables of some sort—but oddly enough, on each coffee table was an enormous candy dish.

From his bedroom window, Oyster had seen such a thing on the counter of the Dragon Palace. When the door was perched wide open, he could make out the cash register and a bit of an indoor fishpond with orange blobs roaming around in it. There was a candy dish on a little stand in between. Oyster understood that someone might want to take a candy after eating a Chinese meal, but in a dentist's office? Candy was the enemy, wasn't it?

On one wall there was a miniature version of the billboard, its smile lit up with Christmas lights. Oyster loved the smile, because it seemed like the smile loved him.

Mrs. Fishback knocked on the glass window for the receptionist, Leatherbelly hooked under her arm.

"Who is it?" a voiced cooed wearily.

"We're here to see Dr. Fromler," Mrs. Fishback said.

The glass window slowly squeaked open, and there appeared a young man wearing a tightly knotted necktie and thick glasses that slid down his beakishly sharp nose. He had very pursed lips as if he were trying to hide his teeth. He puffed his cheeks, too. Oyster wondered what he'd look like if he weren't making such a

strange face. "Dr. Fromler is in a fragile state," he said, the words coming out weird as they were forced through the narrowed gate of his mouth. "With the Awful MTDs, business is down. See the empty office? He's upset about it. You'll have to be very nice to him!" He stared out at them blankly, as if he couldn't see a darn thing.

"I don't care about all of that," Mrs. Fishback said. (She wasn't just rude to Oyster, you know. She was rude to all people. If you're going to be rude, you should at least dole it out equally and fairly, I suppose.) "This is Oyster R. Motel for his appointment."

"Motel, you say? Odd name."

"It's a stupid name," Mrs. Fishback said, staring at Oyster. "But that's why it suits him."

The receptionist jumped up from his seat, disappeared from view for a few minutes, then opened the waiting room door and said, "Can I also offer other products? Dr. Fromler has designed a special line of Mind and Body Products." He launched into an incantation of the familiar small print on the billboard. Oyster mouthed along with him, almost like a little prayer he'd memorized. "Brain Enhancer Tablets, Mr. Pumped-Up Muscles Nose Spray, Child-Calming Menthol Drops; plus: High-School-Diploma-In-a-Bottle Kit, Fishing and Hunting Licenses, and Coupons for Hair Weaves?"

"No," Mrs. Fishback was saying all along, "no, no, no, no." But then she stopped. "Go back," she said.

And so the receptionist listed in reverse: "Weaves Hair for Coupons and, Licenses Hunting and Fishing, Kit Bottle-a-In-Diploma-School-High; plus Drops Menthol Calming-Child . . ."

"Right there! What's that?"

"These Menthol Drops were specially designed for the ornery kid, the rambunctious, hyper, wild, irritating, annoying, overly energetic, ants-in-your-pantsy child who grates on the nerves of all adults in a three-hundred-foot radius."

"Well," said Mrs. Fishback, "at least until I can convince them to get rid of him, those will do. We'll take some!"

The receptionist was very pleased. "Excellent. You won't be disappointed. These drops render a child listless and dull. Guaranteed!"

"Listless and dull?" Oyster asked, hoping the terrified squeak in his voice wasn't noticeable. That it sounded awful, like that time he'd thunked his head while climbing out from under the altar during a sad game of hide-and-seek, where he was the hider *and* the seeker.

The receptionist shoved a six-pack of menthol bottles at Mrs. Fishback. "I'll add these to your bill!"

Mrs. Fishback shoved five in her pocketbook and one into Oyster's pocket—not the one with his map—no, no—the other pocket, luckily. "You'll take these on the ride home!" she said smugly.

"Your boy needs to go to room number one," the receptionist said.

"He's not my boy," Mrs. Fishback said, and then she leaned in confidentially. "He's a reject left on a stoop in the middle of the night," she said in a hushed voice as if Oyster weren't right there. "And he's rotten. It's hard to say what came first: whether he's rotten and so he was rejected or whether he's rotten because he's a reject." She sighed, perplexed by the whole thing. "The only certain thing is that he's a reject."

The receptionist shook his head sadly. "A reject. Rotten, too. What a shame."

"I should go in with him," Mrs. Fishback said. "He's got sticky fingers. Liable to steal anything."

"No grown-ups allowed back!" the receptionist said through his battened-up mouth, pushing the heavy glasses up his nose. "No, no. That wouldn't do at all! Those are the rules! Children need to decide the fate of their smiles."

"But I must ask the doctor about something important." She looked at Leatherbelly, her prince with the crooked teeth. "I need to!"

"Well, you can't go back!" he said sternly. He looked at Leatherbelly too, clasped in Mrs. Fishback's arms, staring but seeing little through his thick glasses. Finally he said, "What an unusual handbag!"

"Thank you," said Mrs. Fishback, turning to Oyster, shoving the dog at him. "You take my handbag back with you. Ask Dr. Fromler what he thinks of it. Ask him!"

Oyster was now holding Leatherbelly. The dog had a paunchy weight, a bum as solid as a bowling ball. "About what?" Oyster said.

"About the handbag's teeth! What else?"

"Does the handbag have teeth? That'll cost extra!" the receptionist said greedily.

Mrs. Fishback shoved Oyster into room one, gave him a stern look. "Just do it!" she said, and then shut the door.

Dr. Fromler wasn't in the room. There was only a black leather chair surrounded by metal arms with various attachments, a small white sink, and a little stool on wheels. Leatherbelly glared at Oyster, panting sourly into his face.

"Why are you looking at me like that?" Oyster asked. "It wasn't my idea to get your teeth looked at!"

Just then the door to room number one popped open and there was Dr. Fromler. Oyster knew that it was Dr. Fromler because he said, "Hello, I'm Dr. Fromler." But, in fact, this man looked exactly like Dr. Fromler's receptionist, except that now he was wearing a white lab coat—so popular among dentists—and no glasses at all, and he was smiling. His smile was as big as the blue merry-go-round horse's teeth and gleaming white. Oyster was momentarily dazed. He blinked into the glittery brilliance of it. *The moon!* Oyster thought. It was as if Dr. Fromler had swallowed it and it was glowing up from his stomach. The smile was pulled back tight, because Dr. Fromler's cheeks were bulging gruesomely. Oyster wondered what they were stuffed with. His packed cheeks made his words come out somewhat garbled. He said, "You like the smile, doncha? I can tell by the glint in your eye."

The glint in Oyster's eye was a reflection of the brilliant smile, which was forcing Oyster to squint. "You're Dr. Fromler?" Oyster asked.

"Of course!"

"You look like the receptionist," Oyster said.

"Did the receptionist have this set of chompers? No, he did not! Only a dentist would have teeth this fine! Plus, receptionists are expensive, and business is slow." He let out an angry huff.

"I like your smile," Oyster said, afraid that the receptionist Dr. Fromler had been correct about the dentist Dr. Fromler being depressed about business.

"Go ahead!" Dr. Fromler said, smiling. "Go ahead and tap 'em. They're solid and white and straight and heavenly! Better than real! Go ahead; give 'em a tap!"

Oyster was scared, mainly of the dentist's big, hard cheeks. But he did as he was told and tapped with his fingernails on the dentist's teeth. They made a high, hollow, pinging noise.

"Beauties, aren't they?" Dr. Fromler said.

"Yes," said Oyster. He didn't like the teeth, though. What were they made of? he wondered.

"Sit up here," Dr. Fromler said. Oyster slid into the seat. "Do you know what I hate?" Dr. Fromler asked.

"No," Oyster said.

"I hate teeth! And you know what I love?"

"No," Oyster said.

"I love candy!" Dr. Fromler pointed to his taut cheeks. Candy! They were filled with candy! Dr. Fromler widened his jaw and let one of the round candies stored in his cheeks slip out into his mouth. He crunched it. Then he quickly opened his desk drawer and fidgeted his fingers till they landed on a big, pink hard candy that he then shot into his mouth, filling the slack spot in one cheek. "I'm smart, boy. I go after the young. Fluoride has almost done me in—that and people brushing their teeth in circles. But if I can convince a child to do otherwise, get him on the right track of bubble gum and—oh, better—hard candies, well, then I've got a customer for life!" He beamed, lighting up the room with an eerie glow. "What's with the dog?" he asked.

"You thought it was a handbag," Oyster said. "With teeth."

"What? The dog? The dog's a dog. Do you need glasses? Are you blind?" He sat down on a little stool on wheels.

"Bad teeth," Oyster said. "Crooked, and his breath is bad."

"Good!" Dr. Fromler was singing it. "Good! Good! Good news, indeed!"

Leatherbelly started and buried his face in Oyster's arms.

Dr. Fromler stuck miniature vacuum cleaner tubes into Oyster's and Leatherbelly's mouths, then scooted around on his little seat on wheels and dug instruments out of drawers. The instruments looked ominous, like small wrenches and mallets.

"A' 'o goin' 'o 'ix my 'oof?" Oyster asked, meaning "Are you going to fix my tooth?" Oyster didn't particularly like the sucking tube in his mouth, and he didn't like the way Dr. Fromler's eyes were staring intently at the instruments. Leatherbelly was growling and biting the tube, wrestling from side to side.

"Fix it?" Dr. Fromler said. (Dentists take special classes in understanding people's speech that's garbled by dentistry.) "No, no, no. Why fix a tooth when I can pull your teeth and put in ones that are better than real?"

Oyster felt his throat close up in fear. His eyes

got wide. He was so scared that he was hugging Leatherbelly. "Wha"?" he asked.

Dr. Fromler was now wearing a green mask over his tight smile and nose. His cheeks still jutted out on either side. He was holding the shiny wrench tool, coming at Oyster with a plastic mask that was hissing out a sinister-smelling fog. "Listen to me, Oyster. Goodies are good. That's why we call them goodies. Keep with them, and you and I will have a long friendship!" Oyster didn't want a friendship with Dr. Fromler. He had before, when Dr. Fromler was a loving smile in the night sky. But not now!

"Just breathe deeply," Dr. Fromler said rather loudly because the vacuum tube had begun blowing air instead of sucking it. In fact, a wind from the sink basin had begun to bluster too. And this time Oyster was happy to hear it. He didn't want Dr. Fromler pulling his teeth. Dr. Fromler himself didn't shine down glittering goodness. He was a fake.

"You'll be asleep in no time! Just hold still!" Dr. Fromler was saying, but Oyster wasn't holding still. He was climbing up the dentist seat with Leatherbelly clamped to his chest, holding on for dear life.

"Get down!" Dr. Fromler screamed.

But the room was gusty now. The vacuum tubes were blowing air with a great force. The windiness from the sink basin was like a tornado. Instruments clattered to the floor. Leatherbelly clawed his way up Oyster's shirt and howled.

Dr. Fromler's white doctor's coat whipped around. The drawers blew open. Goodies shot out and rained down like hail.

There were loud knocks on the door to room one. Mrs. Fishback screeched, "Leatherbelly! Are you okay? Oyster R. Motel, this is all your fault!"

But now the sink basin had opened wide, and from Oyster's perch at the top of the leather chair, he could see that its center had gone black and from the blackness the silver bucket was swinging toward him. Oyster, still holding Leatherbelly, grabbed the bucket just as the door flew open to reveal the fuming, winded, and windblown Mrs. Fishback. Things wouldn't get better if he stayed. He'd be forced to take the Child-Calming Menthol Drops, and he'd be rendered listless and dull, guaranteed! And Dr. Fromler, battling gale force winds, was still after his teeth.

Oyster held tight to the edge of the bucket and jumped for the black hole of the basin. The sink basin's drain widened so that Oyster and Leatherbelly slid through, then fell into darkness. Dr. Fromler and Mrs. Fishback charged the sink basin. And Oyster, bucket in one hand, Leatherbelly in the other, could see their horrified faces, peering down into the drain.

Oyster wedged his bottom into the silver bucket. The bottle of Child-Calming Menthol Drops in one pocket, the small map of his imagination in the other, Leatherbelly in his lap, Oyster was carried off somewhere by the bucket. He and Leatherbelly sailed through darkness.

CHAPTER 5
THE SILVER BUCKET IN THE WELL
(BONELAND WEST OF THE PINCH-EYE MOUNTAINS)

Oyster heard the distant, rustling voices again.

"Get him, Hopps!" one said.

"No, no, there. Hold steady!" said another.

Then the bucket slammed down so hard that Oyster and Leatherbelly shot out. They both ended up sprawled across a floor. It took a moment for Oyster's eyes to adjust. He was on his stomach in a small room filled with cans and barrels marked FIGS: REFRIGERATE. It was dusty and dark. Leatherbelly looked at Oyster as if it had been Oyster's idea to fall through a dentist's sink into darkness, fly in a silver bucket, and land in this cluttered room.

Oyster rolled onto his back and looked up. Two faces loomed over him. One of the faces was small and sweet with blinky eyes. He was smiling as he said, "I think we've got ourselves the right one, don't you?"

The other face, which had a deflated look as if it had once been fat and dimpled, wore a curdled expression, and its beady eyes stared at Oyster suspiciously. "I'm not so sure," he said.

"Oh, Hopps," the happy face said. "It's the boy! It is!"

"Listen, Ringet, we can't jump ahead of ourselves."

So these were the voices that Oyster had heard through the glove compartment. He stared up at them. He wanted to be the boy they were looking for. He wanted to think that all of the strange things—the Awful MTDs, the Mapkeeper, the chocolate on the broom handle, and the silver bucket—were leading to something. But Oyster had trouble believing that he really could be the boy they were looking for. "I'm just Oyster from the nunnery," he found himself saying. He was just Oyster who got in the way and who wasn't worth the trouble.

"Oyster?" Hopps repeated. "That doesn't help!"

"It's the boy!" Ringet went on.

"How do you know, Ringet? How do you know anything?" Hopps said.

"I just do!" Ringet answered. "He was near the spot you left him! He didn't wander too far maybe because he knew we'd be coming back for him."

"I'm not allowed to wander far away, ever," Oyster said. "I'm not allowed outside the nunnery gate except for certain reasons."

Hopps ignored Oyster and lit into Ringet. "I told you that I don't really remember where I left him. That's the problem!" Hopps said, rearing back and poking Ringet in the chest. "And if you breathe a word of that, I'll kill you, Ringet. I will, and we won't be friends anymore!"

It was clear now that the two men were very small, with broad chests and short legs. They wore earrings all the way up their ears and had furry cheeks but bare chins. They both had a good number of dark moles on their faces. They wore flat, circular caps.

"I won't tell," Ringet said. "I've already promised! I haven't even told Oli or Marge or anyone on the Council! But, but"—and here it seemed like Ringet was trying desperately not to say what he was going to say next but he couldn't help himself—"why didn't you mark the spot on the Slippery Map when you got out? Why didn't you?"

Slippery Map? Oyster's cheeks and ears went hot.

"You were supposed to take the baby through the Slippery Map and then leave him there safely," Ringet went on, "and mark it when you got back. It was what his parents wanted!"

Oyster's mind had snagged on the word *parents*. How could he be the boy they were looking for? Maybe slippery maps weren't as unusual as he'd thought. After all, there had been an entire room filled with them. "Stop it, Ringet! Stop it!" Hopps said. "We've got real work to do if this is the boy."

"I don't have parents," Oyster explained. "I was rejected. I'm a reject."

Hopps said, "What's your full name?"

Oyster wasn't sure he should answer any questions now. He didn't want to be belched back into the dentist's office and the clutches of Mrs. Fishback. Plus, Alvin Peterly hadn't answered any questions unless he

was given chocolate. And Oyster could smell the chocolate now. He propped himself up on his elbows and
took a deep breath. He could smell the scent of the
pink chocolate he'd plucked off of the broom handle.
He could see the vats that Alvin had been talking
about. Their rims were crusted in caramel and different
shades of chocolate: blues, greens, pinks, and reds, and
one filled with bright silver icing.

"He's stopped answering," Ringet said.

Leatherbelly waddled off to the corner, walked in
circles, and whined.

"I don't know what that beast is," Ringet said, looking at the dog. "Did you see any of them when you
were there?"

Hopps shook his head. "Don't get too close," he said,
and then he turned his attention back to Oyster.
"What's your full name again?"

Oyster decided he could ask questions just as easily as
answer them. He had plenty of questions. "Where am I?"

Ringet was pleased that Oyster was responding, and
bounced a little up and down. One of his legs didn't
work properly, though, and so it was a rigid bounce
that set him off-kilter. He had to catch his balance.
"You're in the storage room of The Figgy Shop!" Ringet
said. "It's Happy Fig Day! Don't you hear it?" Ringet
pointed to the door.

A bright slice of light slipped into the room underneath

it, and now Oyster could hear people shouting, "Two pounds four!" and "I was next!" There were bells being rung and whistles and singing and drums.

"Only celebration us Perths are allowed, you see," Ringet explained.

"Perths?" Oyster asked. "What are Perths?"

"We're Perths! That's what," Ringet said. "Hopps chose to keep trying, even on Happy Fig Day. At least this way all of the noise and commotion of the celebration blocks out any shouting in here. Any screaming and whatnot. Sometimes they scream, you know."

"Who screams?" Oyster was alarmed.

Hopps didn't let Ringet go on explaining things. "You're in Boneland, just west of the Pinch-Eye Mountains, about three miles to the Bridge to Nowhere and beyond that. . . ." He paused.

"Don't," Ringet said. "There's no need to discuss it now."

"I answered your question; now you answer mine," Hopps said. "What was your name . . . one more time?"

"Oyster R. Motel," Oyster said. He pointed to Leatherbelly, who looked completely dazed and dizzy now from walking in circles. "That's Leatherbelly. And you"—he pointed to the chubby one—"are Ringet. And you"—he pointed to the angry one—"are Hopps. I heard you two talking in the nunnery van."

"*Nunnery*. Second time you've said that word." Hopps walked over to a large scroll of a map spread out on the floor near shelves of canned figs. It was hand-drawn—much like the one in his pocket—with different colored inks, but this one was hugely detailed. There were shop names and treetops and ripples drawn into a river. Both ends of the map were rolled up on cane poles. Hopps walked to the silver bucket with the fancy molding; and once he put his hand underneath it to lift it, the bucket shrank and shrank until it was just the size of a small charm on a necklace. Hopps took the rope, which had become string, and tied it around his neck while poised over the map on the floor. "The nunnery," he said again.

"That's where I live," Oyster said.

"I don't remember anything like that. Nunnery?"

"What do you remember?" Oyster asked, not really sure what his question meant.

"Well, I remember slicing a hole in the Map with the edge of this." He held up the tiny silver bucket. "And then I enlarged it and climbed in with the baby boy tucked in my jacket."

Ringet interrupted. "This was at the height of the Foul Revolution. We had to work quickly. It was dangerous. The baby boy was in danger. Terrible. It was terrible. And it still is!"

"The Foul Revolution?" Oyster asked.

"Dark Mouth," Ringet whispered. "Dark Mouth took over."

Hopps ignored them. He was remembering as best he could. He spoke firmly, trying to nail down the details in his mind. "I went through the Map at night and found myself and the baby in a bed with white sheets and furry floors and an awful painting of a waterfall. When I walked out of the bedroom, I realized I was in a row of bedrooms in a building full of bedrooms."

"A motel?" Oyster asked. "That's what that's called." It made him think of the Royal Motel, and the towel he'd been found wrapped in as a baby.

"I don't know what it was," Hopps said.

"Was it fancy?"

"No, it smelled of wet dogs and socks and standing water."

"Oh," Oyster said, disappointed. It couldn't have been the motel that was part of his birth story. His had been the *Royal* Motel. It had been fancy, with inscribed towels and all.

"I walked the streets of this Baltimore City, holding the baby. There were automobiles and red dots blipping across the night sky. The river was skunky, and they seemed proud of their sugar in Baltimore because it was lit up in a big red sign. There were paddleboats all locked up for the night, and people walking around, shouting happily. I walked away from the river and finally found what seemed to be a good spot. Across the street, there was a red dragon painted on a window."

"A red dragon?" Oyster asked. "Are you sure it was a dragon?" He thought of the Dragon Palace.

"Yes, it was, and I thought, *They know Dragons here— though there's no such thing as a red Dragon. But this is good. He'll learn.*"

"Are there dragons *here*?" Oyster asked quickly.

"Shhh," Ringet whispered, "let him talk." It was clear that Ringet had never gotten this detailed a version of the story before.

"And there was an open window over the red Dragon," Hopps went on. "And through it was a woman holding a baby. The baby cried, but then it stopped and I heard her singing. And that seemed good too."

Oyster thought of the boy across the street with the leg braces. A boy about his age who'd once been a baby . . . Oyster's heart pounded in his chest.

"There was a trinket shop too, with a little puppy sitting there at the front door, looking out at me, wagging its tail."

"A puppy?" Could it be the same mean old dog ten years younger?

"And," Hopps went on, "there was a smiling face in the sky. I can't explain that, but it was there. And it was smiling down on this big stone house."

"A smile? Did you say a smile?" Oyster could barely hear Hopps. He felt light-headed. He patted the Child-Calming Menthol Drops in his pocket. They were still there, although Dr. Fromler's office already felt like a dream. "Like a billboard?"

"What's a billboard?" Ringet asked.

Hopps ignored the questions. "There was an iron gate in front of the stone house. In front of the gate, there was a glowing button and a sign that read: *Please leave deliveries here. Ring bell. God bless.'* Well, that's what I did. I left the baby there and rang the bell and left. I scratched at the curb with the sharp silver bucket to make a hole. The bucket grew. I got in and slipped back through the Map to the storage room."

Oyster could barely speak. Was he the boy they were looking for? "Did you steal something from the motel?" he asked. "Did you wrap the baby in something to keep him warm?"

Hopps nodded. "It was early spring. Still cold. I took a towel," he said. "I didn't want to steal it! I had to!"

"And did you put the baby in something when you dropped him off?"

"I did. Yes, I remember that now, too. I'd taken a crate from some garbage beside a restaurant."

"A Dorsey's Pickled Foods box?" Oyster asked, his voice hoarse.

"Yes, yes!" Hopps said. "I believe it was!"

Oyster could barely speak. He whispered, "And was the towel written on?"

"Yes," Hopps said. "I remember that now, too. Red lettering."

Ringet said, "You're the boy! Aren't you?"

Oyster was crying. He couldn't answer. He was the boy, and he didn't know what it meant. He didn't know where he was. He was coming home, though, wasn't he?

Hopps looked about to cry, too. His bare chin quivered. He said, "I never told anyone this, but I cried here in the storage room after I'd left you, because I was sure I'd never see you again. I was sure that I was going to die and that all of the Perths were going to die, and that you would survive, but I'd never live to see it. That's why I forgot to mark the spot on the Slippery Map. I was too overcome by sadness, too sure that no one would ever find you again."

Ringet looked up at Hopps. He said, "But you *have* lived, Hopps—and so have I."

"And . . . ?" Oyster was afraid to finish the question. "And?"

But Hopps knew what he was going to ask. "And so have your mother and father, even though they're still prisoners. They're alive."

CHAPTER 6
A Buzz in the Ears

Oyster was barely able to understand what Hopps had said. He sat there staring at the canned figs and the chocolate crusted on the lip of one of the vats. He looked at Hopps and Ringet and wondered if they were real or not. Then there was the map still spread on the floor—proof of some sort that this was all real. There was a deep buzzing in his ears. Ringet was touching his shoulder. His mouth was moving, but Oyster couldn't make out the words. Ringet's narrow face was all pursed with worry.

Ringing in his head was the echo of Hopps's words: *They're alive. They're alive. They're alive.*

Then Oyster heard the voices in the fig shop, and everything seemed real again.

"Should I get you water?" Ringet was asking. "Do you need to lie down?"

"I'm fine," Oyster muttered. He was working through it all in his mind. He had questions, thousands of them. But he had to proceed in an orderly fashion. He said, "Prison? Did my parents do something wrong?"

"Oh, he's speaking again!" Ringet said.

"Your parents are heroes!" Hopps said.

"Really?" Oyster asked. He wasn't sure what to think of them. He'd always thought of them as the people who'd abandoned him, who'd left him on a stoop in a box. He'd wanted to imagine that they were good people, that he might one day be with them in a backyard with a swing set, but heroes? Was that possible?

Hopps was rolling up the Slippery Map and becoming all business again. When he lifted the Map, Oyster saw two names on the ends of the poles, white labels like those in the Mapkeeper's shop. He inched closer and made out two names: WARBLER and MIGHT. "This map was stolen," he said.

"It's not stolen! It's your parents' map. It's our origin!" Ringet said with solemn pride. "They made us, you know. They created this World as children, and then they joined us."

"My parents are Warbler and Might?" Oyster asked.

Ringet said, "Yes, and you have to save them!"

"Save them?"

"Well, there's much to do now," Hopps said. "Much to do." He slipped the Map into a leather bag on rusty wheels. "And it won't be simple. Not simple at all. We'll need Ippy, and to find her we'll have to call an emergency meeting of the Council, and we'll have to find Ippy."

"You said that," Ringet muttered.

"Who's Ippy?"

"Hurry now; stand up!" Hopps said. "We've got to get going."

"Now?" Oyster asked.

"Well, no, first you need to look like a Perth," Ringet said. He took out some coal from his pocket and rubbed it on Oyster's cheeks.

"If they knew you weren't a Perth, well, they'd know that you were here for an uprising," Hopps said, fluffing Oyster's hair to hide his unpierced ears. He wrapped a black cape around Oyster's shoulders and fitted a circular cap on his head. "Your parents are too dangerous for Dark Mouth to let them loose."

"My parents are dangerous?"

"In the best way," said Ringet.

What did they mean by *dangerous*? What did they mean by *heroes*? Oyster knew that he was supposed to be happy that his parents were good people after all, but still there was something gnawing at him. Did

heroes—even the dangerous-in-the-best-way kind—
hand over their baby to be shoved through a map and
left on a stoop? These thoughts were just starting to
bubble up, but he didn't know how to ask them.
Instead, he asked, "Who's Dark Mouth?"

"Never mind about him now," Hopps said.

Ringet shook his head, the earrings on his lobes jin-
gling. "But he's after the Map! The boy should know
that he's going to be a target—if word gets out he's
here. Dark Mouth will know he's come through the
Map. He'll know it still exists."

Ringet and Hopps stepped back and looked at
Oyster. Hopps said, "Well, hopefully you look enough
like one of us that you fit in, Oyster, and maybe the
Goggles won't look too closely."

"Goggles?"

"Yes, and be quiet around them. Don't look at them!"
Hopps said. Oyster didn't have much time to ask questions. "Are you bringing the beast?"

Oyster looked at Leatherbelly, who'd squatted and
was now peeing in a corner. "Leatherbelly," Oyster
sighed.

Leatherbelly looked up and trotted to him, dragging
his belly across the floor.

"Are you going to growl at me?" Oyster asked.

Leatherbelly looked up at him and whined sadly.

The dog shook his head.

Oyster scooped him up. "I guess I'll bring the beast," he said.

And with that they opened the storage door into the noisy brightness of The Figgy Shop.

CHAPTER 7

GOGGLES

There were so many people inside The Figgy Shop that Hopps could barely open the storage room door. The Perths were jammed in, their pudgy elbows and doubled chins jutting everywhere, shouting out their orders all at the same time. Oyster had never heard so much shouting in his whole life—he was used to an occasional wheezing from Sister Hilda Prone to Asthma, a cough, and an occasional harumph—but mostly he was used to silence.

"Two pounds four!" an old lady called out.

"Don't push with your pinky on the scale! Don't cheat me!" someone else hollered.

A man and a woman bustled behind the greasy counter, slapping down oily brown bags of assorted figs, collecting coins as fast as they could. Oyster read the names stitched into their Figgy Shop aprons: Oli and Marge. Marge glanced down quickly at Ringet, Hopps, and Oyster, and peeking out behind Oyster's cape, Leatherbelly. She poked Oli in the ribs. He wiped his figgy hands on his apron. Oyster kept an eye on Hopps, who was pulling the wheeled leather bag in which the Slippery Map was hidden. The wheels weren't steady, though, and the leather bag shimmied around wildly. Hopps held one finger to the side of his nose. Ringet looked at Oli and Marge, who put their fingers to their noses for a brief moment.

"They've got it," Ringet said to Hopps over the shouting customers.

Hopps started pushing his way through the crowd more vigorously. "Are the Goggles eyeing us?" Hopps asked.

"No, no," Ringet said.

"What's a Goggle?" Oyster asked.

"Up on the counter, didn't you see him?" Ringet asked. "Don't look!"

But Oyster was already looking. There on the counter sat an enormous toad, eating chocolate-covered figs, tossing its fat-eyed gaze around the store. It was a puffed toad, with skin as shiny as sausage links and webbed feet with sharp claws. The toad's roving eyes fell on Oyster. The Goggle lifted its chest and glared, looking like it was ready to strike. Oyster felt paralyzed with the Goggle's eyes locked on him, but then, for no reason at all, the Goggle broke his gaze and went back to his chocolate-covered figs.

Oyster felt his muscles loosen. Ringet and Hopps were standing in the open doorway.

"Don't lag behind!" Hopps said angrily, stepping outside. "We don't have time for it!"

"I was worried," Ringet said.

"I'll keep up," Oyster said. "I promise."

Hopps and Ringet bickered over the best route to take. Outside, it was evening, and the streets were packed with bustling Perths. The air was humid and warm, but a white dusting of what looked like snow lined the streets and awnings and the limbs of a few puny, beaten trees. Leatherbelly sniffed at the white stuff. Oyster reached down and touched it. It wasn't cold. It was dusty, and it made his fingers white when he rubbed them together. "What's this?" Oyster asked.

Hopps and Ringet looked up. Ringet looked desperately sad all of a sudden.

Hopps answered angrily, "The Devil's Snuff, that's what it is. We breathe it in till we die. How many of us with White Lung Disease now, Ringet? How many kids lost to Powder Pneumonia? And all for what?"

Leatherbelly was licking the powder now, his wet tongue picking it up off the street.

"Don't," Oyster said.

"It won't hurt to eat it except that it's nearly the only thing we can eat. Haven't you noticed the roundness of Perths? Didn't used to be so. I've stopped lapping it up. Stopped as well as I can. You know why people love The Figgy Shop? Well, because there's a fig in it!"

"I don't like figs," Oyster said. "I'd only eat the chocolate coverings."

"Not if you were only given sugar to eat all the time. This powdered sugar is crammed into every bite: noodles, bread, ricey pies. You're not allowed to make anything without sugar as the number one ingredient," Hopps said. "It comes from those." He pointed to the distant skyline. Towering smokestacks puffed white clouds. "They're not spouting as much as usual because of the holiday, but you watch: tomorrow the workers for the morning shift will file in—the whole town almost—and the powdered sugar will be snowing down day and night."

In the white clouds, Oyster read a blue sign: ORWISE SUSPAR AND SONS REFINERY.

"Dark Mouth runs it. He is one of Orwise Suspar's sons—the only Suspar remaining," Hopps whispered; and he glanced over his shoulder in the opposite direction, where a valley of dark woods stood before the Pinch-Eye Mountains. On the very top, Oyster could see a huge torch, a fire burning, smoke furling into the sky. "That's where he lives. As long as the Torch is lit, he's alive and rules over us."

"As long as he's alive . . . ," Ringet repeated.

"Not now," Hopps said. "Goggles." He peered around. "This way." He started off toward the valley, and the others followed along. Hopps muttered under his breath, "Spies! Traitors! Those Goggles used to be on our side during the Foul Revolution, but now they've gone over to Dark Mouth."

"They'll be in the alleys today," Ringet said. "Happy Fig Days, they're afraid of us rising up! And we could rise up, you know! We could!"

"Stop it, Ringet. You'd never have the courage to rise up!"

"Not true! I would if everyone else would!"

"That's just the problem," Hopps said.

The Perths all seemed to be in a rush. They were yelling to one another to hurry and dodging into their small row houses.

"Where are they all going in such a hurry?" Oyster asked.

"It's nearly six. Time for the *Vince Vance Show*," said Ringet. "Perths can't get enough of the 'Home Sweet Home' campaign."

"Brainwashing!" said Hopps. "It's all Brainwashing!

Television belongs to Dark Mouth. Don't let anyone tell you different!"

"I think Vince Vance is very funny," Ringet said gingerly. "And 'Home Sweet Home' programming is nice."

"Nice isn't what we need," Hopps said.

Oyster saw a small troop of Goggles who seemed to be staring at him from under boarded-up marquees. He looked away as fast as he could, afraid one might lock eyes on him and freeze him like in The Figgy Shop. He saw more of them peering out of windows from an office building, another group squatting by a gutter grate. "Hopps," he whispered.

Hopps didn't stop. His wheels kept bumping along the brick path. "What is it?"

"Goggles. They're everywhere."

Ringet swept his head around. "He's right. There are too many of them. They're waiting for someone. They're going to pounce!"

"Ippy'd know how to handle them," Ringet said.

"Who's Ippy?" Oyster asked.

"She is the daughter of your parents' best friends. Your parents—the high leaders—were best friends with two Perths, Fertista and Pillian. You and Ippy were both born during the Foul Revolution. Your parents lived and hers didn't. She lives mostly underground," Ringet explained. "You know about her?"

Oyster shook his head. "No."

"Of course not!" Ringet told himself. "How could he know about Ippy?"

"She's my age?" Oyster asked.

Ringet nodded.

Oyster wondered if Ippy would be his first real friend, someone his own age, someone he could tell secrets to, confide in. Just then a Goggle lifted his head in the air, nostrils tensing in the breeze.

"It's us!" Oyster whispered, nodding toward the Goggles. "They know you have the Slippery Map."

"They don't know," Hopps told him. "They don't know a thing. Frog brains. Don't forget they've got frog brains! Fat frog brains. Don't be afraid. They sense fear. Just keep walking."

Leatherbelly trotted nervously beside Oyster's ankles. "Just act natural, Leatherbelly," Oyster said. "They sense fear."

Just then a young Perth, a woman pushing a baby stroller, came toward them. She was pushing along hurriedly, a Goggle thumping along behind her.

"Don't look," said Hopps.

Ringet grabbed Oyster by the arm. "Oyster, turn away!"

Oyster tried not to look, but he couldn't help it. The young woman started to run, pushing the stroller. Her circular cap flipped off of her head. Now other Goggles hopped out in front of her. They blocked her path, and she stopped, breathless. One Goggle flashed his long tongue, then hissed and reared up, his claws extended. The woman pushed her stroller at them, trying to edge them back, but the Goggles circled tighter. Ringet was now pushing Oyster past the scene.

"Poor thing," said Ringet.

"Aren't you going to help her?" Oyster asked.

"Keep walking," said Hopps.

One of the Goggles knocked over the stroller. It was empty. The woman started to cry. "There was a baby. I dropped her at my mother's. I wasn't transporting goods. I'm not a traitor!" She couldn't move. The Goggles had paralyzed her.

Ringet hesitated. "She's a member, you know, Hopps."

"Pretend you don't know her, Ringet," Hopps said nervously. "Just move along. We have things to do."

"You know her?" Oyster asked.

Ringet didn't answer. He stumbled forward on his locked leg.

"What will happen to her?" Oyster asked.

"She'll go missing," said Hopps.

"Like Oli and Marge's boy," Ringet said quietly.

"We've got to help," Oyster said, and he peeled out of

Ringet's grip. He shouted to get the Goggles' attention. "Leave her alone!"

The Goggles turned, but before they could lock eyes with Oyster, he started to run. He ran downhill, and the clawing Goggles took off after him.

Ringet, Hopps, and Leatherbelly weren't sure what to do. They followed the Goggles, Hopps dragging his leather bag with its wobbly casters, Ringet striding over his locked leg, and Leatherbelly jouncing behind.

"Who was that?" the woman yelled. "Who saved me?"

Oyster opened his black cape in front so that he could run better. *Frog brains,* he was thinking. *They only have frog brains.* He turned down an alleyway so packed with metal garbage cans that there was nowhere to run. And so he climbed on the cans and leaped from one to the next—as he had the chapel pews. The Goggles followed. He could hear their claws clanging against the metal lids.

And he could hear music rising from the glowing windows. Each house's television was tuned to the same theme song. And then there was rousing applause. Oyster took a left at the end of the alley and headed downhill. Before the Goggles emerged from the alley, he slipped into an open front door and shut it.

There was a family of Perths all huddled around the television, eating noodles from a bowl. They turned and looked at Oyster. He put his finger to his lips, and they all listened to the leaping Goggles thudding by on the street. The family looked cozy in the blue light of the TV, and they made Oyster think of the word *parents*. He had a set of those (albeit dangerous parents in jail). He had a family that, if they had the chance, might not be too much unlike this one, eating noodles in front of the television.

Oyster glanced at the television. A Perth with blue eyes was talking into a fat, silver microphone. His hair was gelled back off of his forehead. His beard was trimmed to two points on his cheeks. His eyebrows were thick, and they drew up in the center, as if stitched together. Most of all, he was tan, and his teeth—well, his teeth would have made Dr. Fromler jealous. "Welcome to the *Vince Vance Show* with the Home Sweet Home Players. I'm your host, Vince Vance!" Balloons fell from the ceiling. A band kicked up.

Something about it all was creepy.

The leaping claws of the Goggles had passed.

"I'm sorry," Oyster said. "Wrong house."

The father of the house stood up. "You sure are in the wrong house, I'd say. And you're not even a Perth, are you?"

The three children circled around him. They seemed like they could be about Oyster's age, but they were small and Perthlike. They stared at him. "What is he?" one asked.

"Well," his father said, "look at his markings, kids. The grossly disproportionately long arms and legs. Someone's drawn on the bearded cheeks. He's got no moles of any kind, and his ears lack any celebration. He's, well, I think, he's a Person—the boy kind."

The mother of the house now stood and looked at him closely. She had a baby Perth on her hip. It was ruddy and gave out a hacking cough that seemed to rattle its ribs. "You're right, I think it is a boy Person," she said.

"Who do you know around here?" asked the father, still looking him over.

"I know two Perths," Oyster said. But since that didn't seem like enough, he added, "and I have parents." It sounded strange to his own ears. "But they're in jail, and I'd like to get them out."

"In jail, are they?" the father asked. He turned to his wife and put his finger to his nose. She did the same. It was the same gesture that Hopps had shared with Oli and Marge in The Figgy Shop. Oyster took this as a good sign. "Did you come here through wind and darkness?" the father asked.

"Well, yes, I guess so," Oyster said. "I rode in a silver bucket. I came through the Slippery Map."

"The Slippery Map!" the father Perth whispered, astounded. "Brigid!" he said to his wife. "Brigid! It's the boy! Through the Map, he's come!"

"Well, you've come to the *right* house, then," the mother Perth said.

The father charged over to a closet, pulled out an overcoat. "And imagine, I wasn't going to go to the emergency meeting tonight. Bullus told me about it in the hardware shop, but I said I was fed up. So many false alarms! I'm Birchard and, my wife, Brigid."

"Oyster. Oyster R. Motel." He remembered that Hopps had mentioned calling an emergency meeting. He suppposed that's where he'd catch up with Ringet and Hopps again.

"Good, Mr. Motel, come with me," he said to Oyster. "I can take you where you need to be."

And with that, he hustled Oyster out of his living room and back onto the streets. The Goggles were gone. Oyster followed Birchard down the twisting streets. The white powder on the streets looked blue in the television light pouring from the Perths' windows. The smokestacks were still coughing up dusty clouds, and, on the other side of the dark valley, Dark Mouth's torch was still lit.

CHAPTER 8

MEETING OF THE
HIGH COUNCIL OF PERTHS

"This place used to be called Arthur and Sons Antiques, but when Dark Mouth took over, everyone lost ownership. So stores are called by simple names," Birchard told Oyster. "This is The Antique Shop, you see. We'll find the High Council of Perths hidden away in here."

"Like The Figgy Shop," Oyster said as they walked in the back door of an unlit store.

"Oh, used to be called Oli and Marge's Fine Figs, but now they just work there. Only Orwise Suspar and Sons Refinery gets to keep its name. Oh, I remember the good old days when Dark Mouth's father was just a wealthy old man on the hill—a wealthy old man with a beautiful garden."

The Antique Shop was dusty and stale and dark. Oyster could make out only the dim shapes of frail furnishings: spindly legs, wingback chairs. They walked softly, but still teacups and Hummels jingled in glass-front hutches.

"Why do they call him Dark Mouth?" Oyster asked.

"Only one Perth saw him and lived to tell. He escaped the prison and fought his way back through the valley. When he made it to his own bed, his family all there, poised, waiting for something, he could only whisper two words: *Dark Mouth*. And so that's what he's come to be called. A Winger spy said that he ate and ate and ate until he'd become a massive, sugar-coated form. Sunken eyes, only a stretched hole for a mouth."

Oyster felt a shiver even though he wasn't cold. Birchard walked to a large, wooden grandfather clock with Roman numerals and a door on its chest. He tapped on the clock's door in a little rhythm: *tappity, tap, tap, tap, tappity, tappity, tap, tap, tap*.

"It's our old anthem," he explained sadly.

After a hesitation, the door opened quickly. Birchard dipped inside. "C'mon," he said.

A handful of steps later, they were in a small basement filled with Perths, both men and women. It was sour and gloomy, the ceiling hunkered low. The young male Perth who'd opened the door nodded at the two of them, but other than that, Oyster and Birchard were ignored. Oyster could hear someone calling for

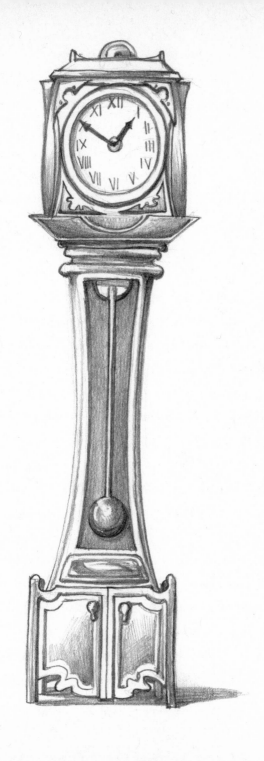

everyone's attention. "Please! Order! Order!"

Someone shouted out, "They've lost the boy? They had him and lost him?" The others hissed and booed.

"Order! Let him talk!"

Oyster could see only an ocean of backs all wearing black coats. Birchard was trying to get someone's attention up front but wasn't having any luck. Oyster tried to jimmy his body through the crowd. Finally he got a narrow view of the front of the room. Ringet and Hopps were standing together on a small platform. Ringet was wide-eyed, wiping sweat from his brow, and Hopps had his hands up. He was trying to explain. "I do have one thing!" he said. "I have one thing that will lead us to the boy!"

"Show us, then!" the crowd shouted out.

"Rah-rah! Hoot-hoot."

"Let's see!"

Hopps bent and lifted up the wide, ample body of Leatherbelly, who stared at the crowd quite dumbfounded.

The crowd hushed. "What is it?" someone said.

"We don't know," Hopps said. "But we assume it's a beast that can find the boy by scent."

Oyster pushed forward some more. Leatherbelly could find only jelly donuts by scent! "I'm here!" Oyster shouted. "It's me. I'm the boy!"

Birchard piped up from the back of the room. "It's the boy! I found him! I did! He came right to me!"

Ringet and Hopps saw Oyster now. "It *is* the boy!" Ringet said, gushing.

"There you go," said Hopps. "And you all doubted me! That will teach you!"

The crowd drew back and split, letting Oyster by. He made his way quickly to the front of the room. The Perths fell quiet. "Is it him?" they whispered. "How can we be sure?"

"I'm the boy!" Oyster stepped up on the platform, facing them.

"Will you save us from Dark Mouth?" someone asked from the crowd.

"I don't know," Oyster said.

"Of course he will. You all know who his parents are. He is going to save them, too!"

There was a small intake of breath from the crowd— awe maybe? Fear? Oyster wasn't sure.

"You should have seen him save the life of Flan Horslip. Flan?" Hopps called out.

And from the crowd, the woman who'd been pushing the baby carriage emerged. Her cheeks were flushed with emotion. "I was coming home from handing out supplies to the Doggers fighting for the valley, and the Goggles were on to me." Her eyes were gleaming with tears. "I was already frozen to the very spot. And then he shouted and got the Goggles running after him. I've never seen anything like it!" she said. "He's the boy, alright. He can take down Dark Mouth. He can put out the Torch! He can start the uprising!"

"Yes," the Perths were chanting now. "Yes, yes!" And, "Rah-rah! Rah-rah! Hoot-hoot!"

"I don't know if I can do all of that," Oyster said. Everyone turned to listen. "I'm just a boy from a nunnery. I'm just a boy found on a stoop in the middle of the night. If I were at home, I'd have taken menthol drops by now and I'd be listless and dull." He pulled the menthol drops out of his pocket, offering proof of his ordinariness.

Ringet said, "But you're our only hope! You must defeat Dark Mouth, and then an uprising would be much much easier, with Dark Mouth gone. Think of your parents!"

"With Dark Mouth gone, you won't need an uprising. There won't be anyone to rise up against," Oyster said.

"Good point," someone cried.

"Rah-rah!" The Perths loved this idea. "Rah-rah! Hoot-hoot!"

Hopps stepped forward. "You've misunderstood the boy. It's like I've been saying. An uprising is something that everyone's got to do. If we all go to Orwise Suspar and Sons Refinery and stand there, instead of working, then there'll be no food for Dark Mouth. We can defeat him if we just refuse to work! That's the uprising right there."

The young Perth who'd worked the clock door yelled from the back, "But what if you say there's an uprising and I'm the only one who refuses to work? We tried it before, and four of us were never seen again."

"That's the truth! My son is gone because of you cowards! You said you were going to rise up, but then you didn't!" It was Marge from The Figgy Shop. Oli stood beside her, patting her arm, trying to soothe her.

"I had the wrong day," one person said.

"Me too. It was confusing," another said.

"I didn't want to cause problems," a third offered.

"You want change with no risk!" Hopps was fuming now. His slack cheeks were red. "That's what's wrong with Perths! So many of us sit at home and love the 'Home Sweet Home' shows and eat our sugar! Don't you see it's all wrong? Dark Mouth is just trying to poison us into thinking everything here is as good as Vince Vance tells us! He's just trying to keep us satisfied with sweetness!"

"But Vince Vance is so perfect!" someone said.

There was a shameful silence. It was clear they'd been over what the group's stance on Vince Vance should be.

"Listen," Hopps said. "I'm only in charge of one

grinder at the refinery. And Ringet is only in charge of lightbulbs. Birchard works in the vats. None of us can shut down the refinery on our own! We all have to do it together!"

"The boy!" the woman who'd been pushing the stroller cried. "The boy can do it! We don't need to! The boy!"

"The boy!" the Perths shouted. "The boy! Rah-rah! Hoot-hoot!"

Hopps settled back, defeated. He turned to Oyster amid the cheering. "I've done what I can with them. You'll have to get the ball rolling, Oyster. They believe in you. I'll help as best I can. Ringet, too."

"I will," Ringet whispered nervously.

Hopps then pulled up a large map like his parents' and tacked it to the wall. He marked an *X* where they were standing. In one direction, there were the smokestacks of Orwise Suspar and Sons Refinery and, in the other, the town of Boneland and, not far off, the Land of the Doggers. Next to it, running parallel, was the Valley of Quick-Eyes, which was spanned halfway across by the Bridge to Nowhere. To get to the Land of Doggers, you had to cross the Breathing River. Both the Land of Doggers and the Valley of Quick-Eyes led to the Pinch-Eye Mountains, the site of Dark Mouth's home, the tower with the Torch on top of it, and, beneath the tower, the prison.

"You forgot to draw the West Coast of Boneland," Ringet said.

"No need. He isn't going out there to look for a tan and sip something by the side of a pool. This is serious business," Hopps said.

"He should use the Bridge to Nowhere for as long as he can," Oli said. "You know, until it ends halfway across, where the fire took it down."

Oyster didn't like the sound of a bridge to nowhere.

"Dark Mouth's Blood-Beaked Vultures have gotten larger," Hopps explained. "They'll pick him off the bridge, and he'll be eaten. I've been looking this over real careful."

Oyster didn't like the sound of the Blood-Beaked Vultures that might eat him. Leatherbelly began doing anxious laps around Oyster's shoes.

"If he takes the tunnels all the way, he can avoid the Dragons, more or less," Marge said.

"More or less?" Oyster asked.

"He can take the tunnels with Ippy," Hopps said. "And she'll know how to keep to the tunnels that the Vicious Goggles don't use so much."

"There are Goggles more vicious than the ones here?" Oyster asked.

"And the Spider Wolves," Ringet said. "Ippy has

killed some of those, I've heard tell."

Oyster hadn't ever heard of a Spider Wolf before, but he liked the idea that Ippy knew how to handle them. "You're sure I'll be able to find Ippy, right? And she'll help me?"

No one answered him. They looked around at one another, sharing anxious glances. Then Hopps just forged on, which didn't make Oyster feel one bit better. Not a bit. "Then he'll break into the prison directly, since he'll be underground. He'll free his parents and then go and fight Dark Mouth."

The Perths said, "Yes, yes," and "Rah-rah! Hoot-hoot!"

"I will?" Oyster asked. "But how do I . . ."

Ringet stared at him with a mix of fear and pride. His wet eyes shimmered.

"You will." Hopps slapped him on the back. "You have to. You're our only hope."

CHAPTER 8½

A BRIEF INTERRUPTION . . .

And what about the nunnery? What about Mrs. Fishback and Dr. Fromler? What about Sister Mary Many Pockets? Their lives don't just come to a screeching stop because Oyster has disappeared, you know.

We left Mrs. Fishback and Dr. Fromler poised over the widened sink basin that opened into a gusty darkness. The sink basin closed after Oyster and Leatherbelly disappeared, and it wasn't long before the television crews were there. Mrs. Fishback loved the camera. She nearly sang to it, "I'm just a simple, kindhearted woman who helps the sweet nuns, and that rotten boy stole my dog and disappeared." Here she pushed up a few tears. "My little prince, my Leatherbelly, my lost dachshund!" And then, as if she'd run out of lines, she started over again from the top. "I'm just a simple, kindhearted woman," she said, "who helps the sweet nuns!"

The camera was quickly turned away from her and on to the glowing teeth of Dr. Fromler. He said, "We here at Dr. Fromler's Dentistry for the Young (and Aged) will be open twenty-four hours a day until the boy and the dog are returned. So come on down and have your teeth fixed while you wait, here, at Dr. Fromler's Dentistry for the Young (and Aged)."

"I will not leave this spot," said Mrs. Fishback, gazing at Dr. Fromler, "until my dog is returned and my teeth are as white as white can be, here, in the care of Dr. Fromler."

And there was a zingy moment between them that even the newscaster could feel in his spine. He cleared his throat and then asked Mrs. Fishback if she could direct them to the nunnery. He wanted to film Oyster's empty spot at the dinner table and Oyster's empty bed. And Mrs. Fishback, all a-twitter with excitement, actually offered, quite kindly, to make a call.

Mother Superior was alone in her office when the phone rang. She picked up. Of course she didn't say anything. She just held the receiver to her ear.

Mrs. Fishback told her the news. "Oyster's had an Awful MTD! He's gone. My Leatherbelly, too!" Mrs. Fishback couldn't even be sad about Leatherbelly at the moment. It was all too thrilling. "And I'm sending the camera crews to you. They want to film you! Imagine that!"

Mother Superior let out a gasp that Mrs. Fishback mistook for joy.

"I know, I know. It's amazing! What a day! I'm staying here with Dr. Fromler! So I'll call you the moment Leatherbelly returns! *If* he returns, that is!"

Mother Superior closed her eyes, put the phone back in its cradle, and cried. Her heart felt like it was cramping in her chest. Their poor Oyster! She rang a bell to call the nuns together.

They clustered in her office, stared into her red-rimmed eyes; and before she even had a chance to write down anything, they started crying, too. They knew that something was wrong with Oyster. Only one nun didn't cry: Sister Mary Many Pockets. She wanted facts. Mother Superior scribbled notes, covering everything she knew. Sister Mary Many Pockets read them as fast as she could; and when she was finished, she raised her hands, asking for the nuns to muffle their sobs. She wrote in thick black marker across Mother Superior's desk calendar in huge letters: WE WILL FIND HIM AND BRING HIM HOME.

The nuns went to the chapel to pray. Sister Mary Many Pockets was among them, there on her kneeler, hands clasped. She was asking, as they all were, for divine inspiration. The nuns were praying so hard that they all broke a sweat, and the chapel smelled like a gymnasium. They would stay there, they'd decided together, praying day and night, with only small necessary breaks, until divine inspiration came to them.

By the time the camera crews arrived, Mother Superior had barred the door, tacking a note below the sign that said: *Please leave deliveries here. Ring bell. God bless.* This one read: *Please leave us be in our time of despair. God bless.*

Jim read the note. "They don't mean it," he said. "Just wait here."

But when he rang the bell and rattled the gate, Mother Superior was waiting. Her jaw was set in steely determination. She handed Jim a note. It read: *We are going to get Oyster and bring him back. We have no time for anything else.*

And then there was Mother Superior's back striding up the walk to the nunnery door. Opening it. Stepping inside. Shutting it.

CHAPTER 9

THE IMAGINATION HAS A LIFE OF ITS OWN

Ringet's apartment was the size of the nunnery's walk-in pantry. And, like the nunnery pantry, it was lined with oversized cans of soup on shelves (*Much too big and too plentiful for one person,* Oyster thought). But unlike the food in the nunnery's walk-in pantry, everything was covered in blue feathers.

"Iglits," Ringet explained, while putting sheets on the sofa where Oyster and Leatherbelly would sleep. "They'd die out there, breathing in all that sugar."

The Iglits were nervous birds. They hid in the rafters, darted around a little overhead. Some perched on the hat rack where everyone had hung his black cape and cap.

"When the factory started up full-tilt, they just fell from the trees," Ringet said sadly.

"Ringet is softhearted," Hopps explained. "Do you

know what these birds would go for on the black market? Fifty skids each, easy."

"I had a bird that I brought back to health," Oyster said, gazing up at the darting birds. "It learned to fly. I can see why people would want these as pets. They're so pretty and blue."

"Not as pets," Ringet said.

"They want to eat 'em," said Hopps.

"How could anyone . . . ," Ringet said.

Hopps leaned into Oyster. "I heard there's an underground recipe for Goggle legs," he whispered. "Now *that* I'd like to try!"

Ringet shook his head and *tsk-tsk*ed. The Iglits on his shoulders ruffled and took flight.

Hopps gave a small laugh that turned into a sigh. He looked tired. "We're all just lucky to be alive. It's worse what happened to the Wingers."

"What happened to the Wingers?" Oyster asked, not having ever heard of Wingers before.

Ringet teared up and walked to the kitchen, busying himself at the counter with bread and jelly jars.

"What are Wingers?" Oyster asked.

"The smallest of Perths," Hopps said. "But they had wings, and when they beat their wings, their chests lit up. Beautiful. But those early days, they couldn't breathe," Hopps explained. "You would find them fluttering on the streets. Their chests dull, just a small glow. Goggles ate most of them."

Oyster imagined the lights flitting out inside of the Wingers' hearts. "That's awful," he said.

"Stop," Ringet called from the kitchen. "I can't think about it. We aren't supposed to be talking about them."

"Right. As Dark Mouth would have it, the Wingers never existed. Nowadays, the kids are raised to believe they were just fantasy stories." Hopps grew angry. "We need our freedom to choose what we think, what we want to do with our lives. We need our history, our past." He sat down at the small table. He lowered his voice and whispered hoarsely to Ringet, "Show him the outlawed books, Ringet."

"No, no," Ringet said. "Hush."

Hopps nodded to the row of soup cans. Oyster looked up at the oversized row. "They won't let us read anything but 'Home Sweet Home' companions. All else is too dangerous."

Ringet shook his head. "Don't look there," he said nervously. "They might see you through a window." Ringet walked to the curtains behind the sink and pulled them tighter. Oyster thought he could feel the Goggles' eyes staring through the darkness outside. He pulled his knees to his chest and sat there in a ball. He could feel his map in his pocket, but he couldn't even remember having imagined that World. It was strange that his parents had invented *this* World! So rich! So fully imagined! So terrifying.

"So why did my parents imagine Goggles and Spider Wolves?" Oyster asked.

"Oh, their own worlds had problems," Ringet explained. "And they couldn't leave all of the old world behind while imagining their own new one."

Hopps went on. "They translated things from the old world into the new; the worlds influence each other sometimes."

"Oh," Oyster said. He had too much to think about. Where were his parents? How would he ever be able to find them, much less rescue them? "I can't save them," he said.

"Sure you can!" Ringet said.

"You saved Fran Horslip," Hopps added.

Oyster was proud of that. Even thinking about it now, he felt a quick smile dart across his face.

Ringet had made some jelly sandwiches and laid them out on the table. Oyster hadn't realized how hungry he was. Leatherbelly got a sandwich too and wolfed it down in a few quick gulps. The Iglits were getting bolder, lighting on the furniture now. Oyster imagined them flying around outside, living in the trees. "What was it like before Dark Mouth?" he asked.

"The Good Dozen," Hopps said. "Twelve years of peace. Your parents had created us, and then found passage to and fro. They would come to visit."

"What were they like?" Oyster asked.

Hopps reached into his pocket, pulled out a wallet. He reached into a zippered compartment and then, within that, a secret compartment. He took out a small picture trimmed to an oval and handed it to Oyster. "There they are," Hopps said.

"I don't know why you carry that on your person!" Ringet said. "It's just too dangerous! If anyone knew . . ."

Oyster leaned in close. The two faces were smiling. The sun was in their eyes, so they were squinting some. His mother had a white veil on her head, and that seemed strange. He realized it was their wedding day; but the veil reminded him of the nuns' veils, and he had a sore heartache—for his parents, squinting into the sun, and for the nuns: he missed them terribly. He was homesick for his home at the nunnery and for the home he'd never known: the backyard with the swing set.

"They were taken from us shortly after you were born," Hopps said. "But they made sure that you were saved."

"But before that, they told us the legend of the land they'd come from," Hopps explained. His eyes were bright, his expression dreamy. He liked this story,

Oyster could tell. "The City of Baltimore in the land of Johns Hopkins in a place called University Housing. Their parents were two sets of professors in this land. And University Housing consisted of damp, old stone homes with fireplaces. They were shushed children, told to be quiet, and with little to do, they made up the story of Perths and the Pinch-Eye Mountains and Boneland. Our origins."

Oyster hadn't spent much time imagining his parents, much less thinking that they'd once been children themselves, about his age, lonesome and bored. He imagined University Housing. It seemed grand, but echoey, a place where it would be easy to get lost and restless—like the nunnery.

"And then one day, while in the dark basement of the library in the land of Johns Hopkins, just west of University Housing, they came across a Map Room and a keeper."

"A Mapkeeper?" Oyster asked.

"Yes," Hopps said. "And the Mapkeeper showed them around her treasures. And among her treasures, they found the map of their own imaginings. As luck would have it, a telephone rang at just that moment. Telephones are communication tools that often make people leave one room and go into another."

"I know what they are," Oyster said.

"Oh, yes, of course," Hopps said. "Well, this is what happened, and they took this diversion to grab their map and run out of the basement of the library in the land of Johns Hopkins and back to University Housing."

"That's what happened to me!" Oyster said. "The telephone and all. Except I wasn't in a basement. I was in a shop!" Oyster thought back to the Mapkeeper, how she'd told him to remember every detail, how she'd given him rules, how she'd told him all about the stolen map—and how loudly she'd labeled the stolen map in bright red pen. Had she meant for Oyster to steal his own map? Had she wanted Oyster's parents in the library basement to steal their own map too?

"Well, it so happens that they ripped the map weeks later. An accident. The girl had a small bucket, an item from a game of some sort. It was on the map, and when the boy accidentally stepped on the bucket, there was a rip. They learned that there was something on the other side of the rip. Wind and darkness. And through that, they found us here."

Oyster thought of his parents as two kids dreaming up their World, and how it must have been for them to come across the Mapkeeper, and that first time when the bucket expanded and the map opened, the two of them sailing through the windy dark. "I am a shushed child," Oyster said. "And I have a good imagination. Except I haven't unleashed mine yet."

Hopps's dreamy expression changed sharply. "What do you mean?"

"You'll need your imagination," Ringet said. "To defeat Dark Mouth."

Hopps said, "Perths aren't blessed with imaginations as strong as humans like yourself have. We need you to make use of yours."

"I'm sorry," Oyster said. He pulled out the map in his pocket, the small scroll he'd stolen from the Mapkeeper. "This is all of my Imagined Other World," he said.

Hopps reached out and took it. He flipped it open on his thigh. "This is it?" His cheeks flushed with anger.

"Yep," Oyster said nervously.

Hopps shook his head and handed it to Ringet.

Ringet took a look. "But here is University Housing. How did you know that?"

Oyster jumped up. "What?" he asked. "Let me see." Ringet handed it to him. His map had a tiny etching of a small square that had the words *The Library of Johns*

Hopkins written beside it. "Maybe I *just* imagined it when I heard about it!" He was astonished.

"He's already improving!" Ringet said to Hopps. "His imagination is inside of him. It's got to be. His parents are his parents, after all."

Hopps looked doubtful, and Oyster squirmed. "I really will try," he said, "to unleash it. I will!"

Ringet took the map, pulled an oversized soup can from a top shelf. "I'll put it here for safekeeping." He dropped the map in the can. It made a hollow *thunk*. The can had no lid. Ringet simply put it on a high shelf.

"Are you sure it will be okay up there?" Oyster asked.

"If it isn't okay up there, then there still really isn't much to lose now, huh?" Hopps said sourly.

For the first time, Oyster really didn't like Hopps. "I guess not. Or well, not yet," he said.

Ringet said, "Look, Hopps, stop it. I have faith in the boy."

Hopps ignored him. "The first dozen years were wonderful. The refinery was operating, yes, but not with all of the heavy pollution, and we chugged along as a quiet town. We held elections and squabbled over our small plots of gardens. We fussed, yes, but we were allowed to fuss. And then we sang all day Saturdays."

"And Orwise Suspar was an old, wealthy man," Ringet said. "The spot where Dark Mouth now has his Torch atop a tall thin tower, it used to be a garden with twenty-foot flowers: High-Tipping Bluebells and Rosy-Upsies. And when the petals fell off, they were as big as bedsheets, and they drifted down into the valley and lay like carpets."

"And now do you want to know what happened after the Good Dozen?" Hopps asked.

Oyster nodded, though he knew it would be an awful story.

Hopps stood up and paced around the little room. Oyster guessed that this was the way he told the hard stories. "The old man in the tower died. And his son decided to *rule* over us. He'd once been a sweet little boy, standing behind his father in photographs; but after his father died, he became evil. The Foul Revolution was upon us—the vicious attacks of Dark Mouth's troops. Your parents fought alongside us. They were our leaders, and they were taken."

"Why did Dark Mouth become evil? Why did he want to rule over everyone?" Oyster asked. "If everything had been going so well?"

"Do you think I understand him?" Hopps said.

Ringet shook his head. "It's not for us to know," he said. "It's beyond us."

"But we have to know," Oyster said. "We have to understand what happened with Dark Mouth or we won't ever be able to make things right."

"Well," Hopps said, a little huffy, "what's there to know? He wants to keep us down like we're just caged Wingers who need to be obedient. He wants the Map so that he can go through it and take over the land on the other side. His greed has no end."

"And he turned his father's beautiful garden to bone. He killed it!"

Oyster didn't like the sound of any of this, but right now, his mind was stalled on a point of logic. "Why didn't my parents just imagine that everything was good again so it would go back?"

"The imagination is its own force. Once you fully imagine something, it is, in a sense, true. It exists. And, once in motion, it takes on a life of its own, Oyster. Your parents created us, but we go on of our own volition— the good and the bad. Your parents were trying to convince us that we have our own imaginations. And we believed them," Hopps said. "But now they're gone and a lot of Perths have lost that belief in themselves. If we could all just imagine a better place here, we could make it ourselves. But I can't convince the Perths of this. They're all too terrified to try."

"Who could blame them?" Ringet said, obviously ter- rified himself.

"And the last thing Dark Mouth wants is for us to go

about having imaginations. He wants to control every-thing. The artists and storytellers—well, they were the first to be imprisoned. Dark Mouth hands us his 'Home Sweet Home' programming and has us eat our sugars and thinks, 'That will satisfy them. Keep them from ris-ing up. Give them enough to chew on.' But it isn't any-thing to chew on!"

"Oh," Oyster said. He didn't understand his imagina-tion himself, except how to keep a lid on it, but . . . Suddenly it was there in his mind: the green lawn and the blue-and-white striped swing set, and his father in a garden with a hose and his mother putting a check-ered cloth on a picnic table, some shirts gusting on a clothesline behind her . . . and he and the boy from the Dragon Palace, still holding his blue umbrella, were laughing on the swings, the wind in their hair. His own Imagined Other World. It was the most he'd ever let himself imagine about that World.

"That's why we need you, Oyster," Hopps said. He spread the Slippery Map on the floor. He said, "Okay, now we won't be here in the morning when you head out. We'll have to head to the refinery early."

"I'm going off by myself?" Oyster asked. "With the Map?"

"You've got the beast," Ringet said.

Oyster looked at Leatherbelly, who was nearly

asleep, his jowls resting on his black paws. "I don't think he'll be of much use to me," Oyster said.

"He's your beast, though," Hopps said.

"He's not a beastly beast, and he's not really mine," Oyster explained.

"If we don't show up at the refinery, it'll alert the Goggles." Hopps took off the necklace of the silver bucket on a string. "Listen. You'll have the Slippery Map, too. When you need us, you take off the necklace." He touched a spot on the Map with the bucket and the Map enlarged in that spot, showing the layout of Ringet's apartment. "Here's the sink. Scratch at it like this." He used the rim of the bucket like a paring knife. There was a small black gash, an opening. A cold breeze poured through it. The wind also kicked up through Ringet's sink, batting around his kitchen curtains. "Talk to us through the wind. We'll be here after five thirty."

"You're giving me the Slippery Map?" Oyster asked.

"Actually, I'm returning it. It belongs to your family," Hopps said.

Oyster again thought of his parents as shushed kids in University Housing. "But," Oyster said, after a little thought, "isn't Dark Mouth after the Map? I mean, won't I be even more of a target if I've got it with me?"

Ringet and Hopps glanced at each other nervously.

"Well," Hopps said, "as a matter of fact, that's true."

Ringet's eyes teared up. "And those Perths at the Council meeting, they're bound to gossip. It's bound to be leaked out!"

"We have no choice now but to go forward," Hopps said. "You'll have to find Ippy first off."

"She'll know how to take you through," Ringet said. "She's the toughest person we know. And she'll help you. She has to!"

There was something about the way Ringet said that she had to help that made Oyster think that she might not help. And what if she didn't? He wasn't sure. "How will I know where to find Ippy?" Oyster asked. He was more than scared. He wasn't sure how to use the Map or if he could make it work. Sister Mary Many Pockets had taught him only a little bit about maps—that the bumpy ones are topographical and that maps have keys and four directions: N, S, E, and W. He didn't want to wander around in this place without a native.

"Ippy lives among the Doggers most of the time," Hopps said. "Go here," he pointed to the edge of the Valley of Quick-Eyes. "That's where Flan was coming from when you saved her. She's got a brother down there. She leaves the food off right here." Hopps pointed to an enlarged section of the map. There was a hollowed-out tree tilting near a river. "After that you'll have to cross the Breathing River to get to Ippy in the valley." He pointed to a winding, gray waterway. "You swim? Know anything about Water Snakes?"

"The nuns aren't allowed to swim," Oyster said. "So I never learned."

"You'll be able to follow the sound of the whining Growsels; they're bog beasts deep in the valley but noisy this time of year," Hopps went on.

"You're the boy," Ringet said with hushed reverence. "You'll know what to do!"

Oyster felt like he'd been lying. These people thought he was someone else, and he'd let them. He'd even said it himself, "I'm the boy!" and maybe at the Council meeting he'd actually meant it. But now he couldn't believe it anymore.

"This isn't right. I mean, maybe I'm not the boy. Really, all I know is that I'm just *a* boy. I'm not really fit for any of this. I collect moths in shoe boxes. I look out windows. That's all. I thought that a billboard of teeth was smiling its love down on me, but I was wrong." And now tears slipped from his eyes. "I'm a reject," Oyster said. "A reject. Mrs. Fishback told me so. I'm just Oyster R. Motel, a stupid name for a stupid boy."

"Oyster, your parents are brave people," Hopps said. "They can't paralyze with their stare like the Goggles.

They can't breathe fire like Dragons. They're not venomous, eight-legged wolves. They have only brave hearts, true hearts, and good imaginations. And when they speak from their hearts and tell us the World that they imagine could one day be the one we live in, well, people are inspired."

"Your parents have led us in the past, and they will lead again," Ringet said. "You, Oyster, are born from them. You have their kind of heart."

Oyster wasn't convinced. "How do you know?"

"You've already saved Flan Horslip," Ringet said. "You've spoken to the Perths at Council. They believe in you."

"They do?"

"Yes," Ringet and Hopps said.

"Oh," Oyster said quietly.

"Give him the silver bucket," Ringet told Hopps.

"Oh, yes." Hopps lifted the silver bucket and placed its string around Oyster's neck. "There you go. Yours now."

Oyster patted the bucket, now as small as a charm. He felt a little better, but mainly he was tired. He put his head down on the sofa and propped up his feet. Leatherbelly curled up on Oyster's stomach. Oyster missed his own bed. He missed his window that overlooked the Dragon Palace and Gold's Fancy Pawn Shop

and Cash Store. He even missed Dr. Fromler's billboard, even though he knew Fromler was a fake. But
most of all, he missed the quiet shushing of the nuns,
the padding of their rubber-soled shoes, the way they
moved around in their bell-shaped black habits; and
Sister Mary Many Pockets—he missed her sorely. He
thought of the times they kicked back from textbooks
and propped up their feet and ate peanuts, how Sister
Mary Many Pockets had shown him the small, dusty
cloud that would sometimes puff right when you
cracked a shell. He knew that she was worried about
him, that she was fretting. He hoped that she wouldn't
be swallowed up in sorrow. But he was needed here in
this strange place. He was the boy.

Hopps was moving the Map this way and that, looking for the best routes, griping about Vicious Goggles
under his breath. And then, at one point, he looked up.
"Who's Mrs. Fishback, anyway?" he asked, to himself
more than to Oyster.

And Oyster was going to say, "Nobody. Just this person I used to know." But he didn't have the energy. He
fell fast asleep.

CHAPTER 10
TALKING THROUGH THE MAP

When Oyster opened his eyes, Leatherbelly was covered in blue feathers, snoring beside him. Iglits were beating lazily around the rafters. He found a note from Ringet on his chest:

> *I've wrapped up extra figs and a small brick of coal in the leather bag so that you'll have something to eat and can keep your cheeks darkened. Be careful, Oyster. Beware. Call us if you need our help!*

Oyster hopped out of bed. Blue feathers drifted to the floor. He glanced around the little room. *Ringet and Hopps,* he thought, *they've already headed off to the refinery for work.* He glanced out of the window. Hopps had been right about the powder snowing down from

Orwise Suspar and Sons Refinery and how it would only get worse. The window was a blur of white, a sugary blizzard.

He looked inside of the bag of figs. Ringet had packed way too many. Oyster didn't even *like* figs. He sat forward on the bed, the bottle of menthol drops digging into his leg. Child-Calming Menthol Drops and figs? And they expected him to defeat Dark Mouth?

Suddenly, he had a heroic idea. He opened the bag of figs and the bottle of menthol drops. He filled the dropper and then wedged it into one of the figs and squeezed, filling the fig with Child-Calming Menthol. He did this to a dozen more of the figs and then got another paper bag out of Ringet's kitchen. He wrote *Menthol-Flavored Figs* on the bag that he'd doctored up. He might be able to defend himself if the Goggles came at him. He could render them listless and dull. In any case, it didn't hurt to have the figs on hand.

Oyster looked at his feet, and there was the leather bag on casters. Oyster knelt, unbuckled it, and looked inside. The Slippery Map was snugly rolled up on two short cane poles, just as Hopps had said.

"Ippy." Oyster said her name out loud. "Today I'll meet Ippy—who will lead me to my parents." He liked the sound of the words *my parents*. He'd never had much of a use for the words before, but now he did. It was still strange to him that he really had parents.

Oyster pulled out the Slippery Map and rolled it out across the floor. He stuffed the figs—regular and menthol-flavored—inside the leather bag. He took off the necklace with the silver bucket and held it tightly in his fist. On the Map, he could see Boneland and, to the west, the edge of the Valley of Lawless Beasts, where he had to go to find Ippy. He looked at the valley below the Bridge to Nowhere and, on the other side, Dark Mouth's Torch. In east Boneland was The Antique Shop, The Figgy Shop, and beyond that, Orwise Suspar and Sons Refinery; and east of that was what Oyster thought was an ocean. But written in tiny, somewhat messy handwriting was this: *The Gulf of Wind and Darkness*. It was kid's handwriting. And Oyster realized that it was either his mother's or his father's when they were little and living on the same street in University Housing, two bored kids making things up.

Oyster rolled the Map to reveal what was on the other side of the Gulf of Wind and Darkness: *The City of Baltimore*. Oyster saw the Inner Harbor ringed with boats, a zoo. Johns Hopkins and University Housing, where his parents had grown up. He recognized the names of streets: Pratt and Charles and, most importantly, York Road. He let his finger drift along York until he came to his very own side street. There he found the

Dragon Palace and Gold's Fancy Pawn Shop and Cash Store, and, of course, the nunnery. Oyster wondered how far the Map would go. It still had a thick roll of paper around each of the cane poles. Did it go to China? Russia? Toledo? Jerusalem? He was curious, but for now, he couldn't stop gazing at one spot: the nunnery.

Oyster knew that it was around the time of morning prayers. He imagined the nuns in the chapel. Were some of them so very happy that he was gone that their prayers were of thanksgiving? Oyster knew that Sister Mary Many Pockets's prayers wouldn't be. She would want him back, wouldn't she? She was worrying. He was sure of it. He could feel her heart talking to his heart about grief and worry.

He put the silver bucket to the nunnery on the Map. The Map widened to include the nunnery kitchen, the pantry, the back stairs to the bedrooms. Oyster led the bucket to the chapel. What would happen if he opened up just the smallest portal through the Map? Maybe he could speak through the Gulf of Wind and Darkness. He wasn't sure if it was the right thing to do or not. But he needed to practice, didn't he?

Oyster used the edge of the bucket like Hopps had taught him, cutting a small slit in the Map. It let out a gust of air. Maybe Sister Mary Many Pockets would be there. Maybe he would be able to tell her that he was okay.

He leaned his head over the gusty hole and shouted, "Hello! It's me! Oyster! I'm okay, Sister Mary Many Pockets! I'm doing fine! Don't worry!" He paused to listen for some sound to come back—a sneeze, a harumph, a screech. For a moment, there was silence, and then he heard something: a low sound and high sounds all at the same time. Some awful music? Was it the old organ that sat in the chapel's dusty corner? Oyster listened as the notes got faster—highs and lows all at the same time. It was the chapel organ; there was no mistaking its loud old wheeze.

The noises woke up Leatherbelly, who started to howl mournfully. This startled the Iglits, who squawked and batted around Oyster's head.

"I'm okay!" Oyster shouted again into the hole, though he didn't sound as sure as he had the first time. "Sister Mary Many Pockets! Are you there? Don't worry! Don't be swallowed up in sorrow!"

As he spoke, the hole grew wider and gustier. When Oyster reared up, afraid he might fall into the darkness again, he saw he was no longer holding a small string. It had thickened into a rope, and the silver bucket was full-size. The organ was playing only one low, mangled chord. It wouldn't let the chord go. The bucket rolled across the floor, as if it had a mind of its own and knew just what to do. It rolled toward the hole. But Oyster

couldn't lose the bucket down the hole. He couldn't! He got up and yanked the rope as hard as he could, making the bucket pop up, fly across Ringet's apartment, and skid along the floor.

He raced to the Map and rolled it up as quickly as he could. This muffled the hole, and it sealed. The wind stopped. Oyster shoved the Slippery Map into the leather bag, sat back on his heels, and sighed. He was breathless, his heart charged and racing.

Did she hear me? Oyster wondered.

Leatherbelly hopped off the sofa and licked Oyster's nose while the Iglits lighted down, staring at Oyster, cocking their bright blue heads.

Chapter 10½

A Brief Interruption . . .

Maybe you're wondering what was happening on the other side of the Gulf of Wind and Darkness, specifically in the nunnery chapel that morning.

It was full, as you know. And Oyster was wrong. It wasn't just Sister Mary Many Pockets who wanted him back. All of the nuns did. They were all praying for divine inspiration when the little lids that sat on top of the organ's pipes burst up with cold air.

When Sister Mary Many Pockets heard Oyster's voice, she ran to the organ and climbed on its keyboard to look for Oyster inside the pipes. Her rubber-soled shoes made a racket on the keys. The other nuns followed and helped her keep her balance. When Sister Mary Many Pockets grabbed the pipe with the most wind blasting from it, the pipe grew wide. She pulled on it and it opened up some more, the organ straining loudly, its notes holding and holding and holding while the nuns supported Sister Mary Many Pockets. She motioned to the nuns: Higher! They made a small pyramid by balancing on the organ bench and keyboard and boosted her up. She pulled the pipe's mouth as wide as it would go and then, with a final hoist from the nuns, she dived in.

Without the silver bucket, without anything to guide her except her love of Oyster R. Motel and a lot of faith, Sister Mary Many Pockets glided and fell and floated through windy darkness.

CHAPTER 11
GROWSELS AND DOGGERS

Oyster and Leatherbelly headed out into the snowlike powder. It was warm, but Oyster still found himself hunching his shoulders as if it were winter. Leatherbelly kept snorting the powdered sugar out of his nose in gruff little grunts, but he liked to stop and lick it, too.

"C'mon, Leatherbelly," Oyster told him. "We've got to keep moving."

Oyster walked with his head down so the Goggles would mainly see the flat cap that he'd secured by tying it under his chin. The streets were mostly empty except for a few people on bicycles, a row of schoolchildren, a crew of workers wearing gray Orwise Suspar and Sons Refinery uniforms sweeping powder into large cans. One time, a shopkeeper peered out of The Repair Shop, stared at Oyster, and put his finger to his nose. Oyster was a little startled. He put his finger to his nose too.

The shopkeeper smiled and disappeared from behind the glass.

Goggles sat at nearly every intersection. The powder collected on their warty backs and flat heads. They gave small, leaping shivers to shake off the powder but always kept their eyes on the streets. Oyster was afraid of them but tried not to be. He didn't want them to sense his fear. They always seemed most interested in Leatherbelly. They watched him trot by, but they seemed to be a little afraid of him and always let him pass.

Oyster was scared that they'd sense the Slippery Map, though he didn't think they had the ability to do that. *Frog brains,* he reminded himself. If attacked, would he be able to get to the menthol-flavored figs? Would he be able to get the Goggles to eat them? Would they actually make the Goggles listless and dull, or did they only work on children?

As he wheeled the leather bag behind him over the bumpy streets, he felt like he was dragging two Worlds with him, not just drawn on a map, but the Worlds themselves and the Gulf of Wind and Darkness between them. He felt like he was hauling everything he knew: Sister Mary Many Pockets in the nunnery and his parents' childhood in University Housing and the Perths' whole existence. It was tiring.

He was relieved when the roads tilted downhill

toward the Valley of Lawless Beasts. The powder wasn't snowing as heavily now that they were farther from the refinery. There were fewer Perths and Goggles, too. Hopps had been right: Oyster could hear whining in front of him. He knew that it must be the Growsels, but he didn't know what Growsels were.

The sidewalk ended in a brittle patch of cement that led to grass and a bank of trees, and the leather bag got harder to maneuver. It pitched over, but Leatherbelly was there, and he helped nose it upright. This surprised Oyster. Leatherbelly hadn't ever been helpful before.

"Thanks," Oyster said.

Leatherbelly looked at him shyly, and they went on.

They followed a worn path and came to the hollowed-out tree where Flan hid food for her brother and the Doggers. Oyster leaned against the tree to look into the pockets of its roots. They were empty. Before he had a chance to step back, the tree began to vibrate with whining. There was a bumping noise inside the trunk so loud that it made the leaves shudder. Oyster yanked on the bag, stepping away as fast as he could. Leatherbelly dodged behind Oyster's legs.

Then burrowing up from the roots of the tree came a thick snout with white tusks—a Growsel, judging by its whine—but it wasn't alone. Holding on to each tusk was a very small, pale, grimy hand. Oyster hid behind a tree, pushing Leatherbelly behind him with one foot. He watched the Growsel work at the dirt and waited for everything to emerge. The Growsel's paws seemed to be making the noise. They were churning the dirt like the rototiller that Sister Theresa Raised on a Farm had once used in the nunnery's back lot.

The Growsel finally popped out of the tree. It had a shiny black coat. On its back sat a very small Perth who wouldn't stand taller than Oyster's knee. He had furry cheeks and a bare chin, but he wasn't wearing a cape and hat. He wore dirty trousers, patched at the knees, and a work shirt. He was between the size of a Perth and the size of the Wingers Hopps had described. But there was nothing delicate about this Dogger as there

had been with the Wingers. He was wiry and lean. Oyster was afraid of him. He rolled to the other side of the tree, then stood as silently as he could.

The Growsel in front of the tree had stopped pawing, but there had to be thousands more burrowing and whining. The ground was alive with them.

"I know you're there," the small Perth said in a rough voice. "Have you stolen something? Are you here to cheat us? Did you think you could just show up and no one would be the wiser?"

Oyster didn't say anything. He didn't move. He could barely breathe. He didn't like being called a thief, because he was sure that it was true. He'd stolen his map, and the deed still weighed on him.

"Come on out," the small Perth said. "Or would you rather I drag you out into the light?"

Oyster peeked from behind the tree. The small Perth had gotten off of the Growsel's back but still held on to one of its tusks.

"Full view," the little Perth said. "Hands on your head too, so I can see 'em."

Oyster put his hands on his cap and stepped out from behind the tree, leaving Leatherbelly and the bag behind.

"And the other one! I smell two of yous."

Leatherbelly gave a sad whine and then tiptoed out.

"Humph," said the little Perth, looking Oyster over first. "You're no Perth," he said. Then he stared at Leatherbelly. "What's this?" He walked up a little closer and sniffed in the dachshund's direction. "You two aren't from here," the little Perth said.

"We belong here, anyway," Oyster said. This land was his parents' creation. That should count for something.

"Doggers know who belongs and who doesn't."

"You're a Dogger?" Oyster asked.

"Proudly, yes." He stiffened up, jutting out his bare chin. "A true fighter. Determined to take back what's ours."

"I know Flan Horslip," Oyster said, trying to sound casual. "I saved her life."

"Flan Horslip? You say you saved her?" The Dogger looked suspicious.

"I saved her from a group of Goggles that had surrounded her," Oyster explained.

"Call those things you got Goggles? Vicious Goggles here will eat your Goggles like a box of fat chocolate figs. Here, you've got to be ten times smarter and faster and stronger." He paused and eyeballed Oyster. "No one comes here without a reason. And I don't know if your reason is friendly or foul."

"I think it's friendly," Oyster said. "I just want to see Ippy."

"Ippy? Ha! You're kidding. You know Ippy? You don't seem like her type—hiding behind a tree! Do you think she'd hide like that? Never!"

Oyster was pretty sure that the Dogger was right. What was he doing here, hiding already? The Growsel started digging nervously, churning up dirt, but the Dogger tapped his backside and he stopped.

"I don't know; I've never met her," Oyster said, again trying to sound braver than he felt. "Her parents and my parents were best friends. I need to see her, though. I've got important, very dangerous work to do. I've got Perths to save and my parents to free from jail."

The Dogger hesitated. "You're saying that you are the boy?"

Oyster nodded, staring the Dogger in the eye.

"You're going to free your parents?"

"Mmm-hmm," Oyster said.

"Do you even know how to find Ippy?"

That gave Oyster pause. "No, not really."

"You can't go it alone," the Dogger said. "Look at you!"

Oyster glanced down and looked at himself. He took his hands off of his head and brushed dirt from his cape. "I just have to do the best I can."

"You're the boy? Really?"

Oyster nodded again.

"And Ippy is going to help you?"

"I think so," Oyster said. "Her parents and my parents—"

"I know, I know; they were friends. You've been over that."

The Dogger glared at Oyster, sharp and mean, examining him. "How'd you break your tooth?" the Dogger asked.

"Too awful a story to tell," Oyster said, shaking his head. "Bad times."

This made something in the Dogger break open. "I know what you mean," he said, showing Oyster a set of scars: one on his eyebrow, one on a thumb, one on his elbow. "C'mon. I'll lead you to Ippy. Follow me," he said.

The Dogger climbed back on the Growsel. Oyster grabbed his leather bag, and he and Leatherbelly followed through the woods. At first there was a soft, hushed distant whisper of breath, but as it grew louder and louder, Oyster knew where they were headed—the Breathing River—and he felt sure that there was no turning back now.

CHAPTER 12

THE BREATHING RIVER

At first the Breathing River sounded only like breaths, thousands of them, rising like bubbles and sighing on the surface. But as Oyster and Leatherbelly followed the Dogger through the woods, the river grew louder, until it drowned out the collective whine of the Growsels underground. And it sounded like the nunnery at night when Oyster would walk down the hall to the bathroom. Some of the nuns snored with puffs, others with rattles, others still with whinnies. In fact, he almost recognized the wheezy snore of Sister Elouise of the Occasional Cigarette, and then the baritone of Sister Augusta of the Elaborate Belches, and then, just softly, just once, the puff of Sister Mary Many Pockets.

"Do you hear that?" Oyster asked.

"It's different," the Dogger said. "It's never quite sounded like that before—more like snoring, isn't it?"

"Strange," Oyster said. "I think I recognize some of those snores."

The Dogger looked at Oyster for a moment out of the corner of his eye.

"What?" Oyster asked.

"Nothing," the Dogger said.

Oyster didn't understand it, but it seemed like his World was here somehow, in those snores. Finally, when the river came into view—a rough, winding, gray river—the noise had risen to a roar. The Growsel stopped at the reedy bank. The Dogger climbed off the back of his Growsel and walked to the edge. He stuck his hand in the water.

Oyster and Leatherbelly hung back, neither wanting to get too close. The Breathing River was fast. Bubbles stirred up and snapped by Oyster's ears: an angry cough, a few sharp pants, another with a whistle, and a moan. Oyster didn't like the river. It was rough, churning briskly over large, sharp rocks. He could see three Water Snakes from where he stood.

"I've got no boat. Only way's to swim. You aren't afraid of snakes, are you?" the Dogger asked with an edge to his tone.

Oyster shook his head. "Nope," he said, although he'd never seen a snake. They didn't show up in downtown Baltimore. He didn't like the looks of the Water

Snakes he did see. But he was still trying to fake some kind of confidence, just a little.

The Growsel nosed up behind Leatherbelly, gave a low growl and a snap. Leatherbelly skidded forward and almost fell into the water. The Growsel snapped again, and Leatherbelly had no choice. He plummeted into the river. He paddled madly. Luckily, it turned out that he was very buoyant because of his paunch. He bobbed along more than he swam. The Growsel was next, his hooves spinning.

Oyster stood there. He didn't want to tell the Dogger he couldn't swim, but he knew that swimming was something he couldn't fake. And even if he could swim, what would happen to the Slippery Map if it got wet?

The Dogger walked into the water, pushing his way in with his tough, muscled frame. He looked back over his shoulder. "What are you waiting for?"

Oyster looked upriver and down, hoping for a bridge, but there was none. Then he looked overhead. The trees were tall and thick, and strung with mossy vines. Oyster jumped up and grabbed hold of one of the vines. It was strong. It held.

"Hurry up!" the Dogger yelled, swimming through the current. "Don't have all day!"

Oyster had a plan. He shouted back, "I'd prefer to stay dry."

"Not possible," the Dogger said. "If it were possible, I'd a-figured it out by now! No time for that!"

Oyster saw two vines that lined up pretty nicely. It would be like pulling the bell in the nunnery bell tower, except he'd be riding one from one church bell rope to another.

The Dogger was nearly to the other side. "You're wasting time!"

Oyster buckled the leather bag to his belt, climbed a tree, scooted out on a limb, picked up a vine, and pulled it closer to the trunk. He then shinnied to the underside of the limb and let go. He soared out across the Breathing River, caught the other vine, released the first, and swung through the air. He could see the Dogger pulling himself onto the bank, the Growsel already there. Both sets of eyes were on Oyster, watching him glide. Oyster rode over the far shore until he dropped, landing right in front of the Dogger and his Growsel.

The Dogger staggered backward a bit. "How did you do that?" he asked.

"I have some skills," Oyster said. This surprised him. He didn't think he had any. "From back where I come from."

Just then there was thrashing in the water: Leatherbelly paddling fiercely, his head dipping under

and then appearing again and then disappearing.

"Leatherbelly!" Oyster called out.

"Too bad about your beast, though. Don't see him." He patted his Growsel. "They don't always make it."

Oyster felt a rise of panic. He hadn't known that he needed Leatherbelly until this moment. He ripped off his shoes, set down the Map, and ran into the water. It was cold. "Leatherbelly!" he called again, not sure which way to try to swim to reach him.

"Can't save him," the Dogger said. "He's been taken down by a Water Snake. Nothing to do for him now."

Everywhere Oyster looked, the Breathing River was bubbling with its sighs and moans and chirps, and he couldn't tell which bubbles might be Leatherbelly fighting underwater. He wasn't ready to give up, though, and even though he couldn't swim, Oyster was poised to dive in anyway.

But right at the last moment, before Oyster had a chance to spring into the river, Leatherbelly popped up and proudly glided to shore, with a long, black Water Snake limp in his mouth.

CHAPTER 13

LAWLESS BEASTS

The Dogger stood on the noisy shore of the Breathing River, his small, bony hands folded on his narrow chest, clearly impressed. "Doggers don't give their names out first off," he said. "They've got to be earned, you know, only given when a Dogger has gained enough faith."

Oyster's wet pants clung to his shins. His socks were soaked. He wondered if the Dogger had gained enough faith or whether he was just teasing him. There was a long pause. And then finally the Dogger said, "I'm Drusser, and this is my Growsel, Tipps."

His hand shot out, and Oyster shook it, feeling very happy. "I'm Oyster, and this is Leatherbelly."

Drusser didn't allow him to dwell on the new friendship. He said, "It's time to go underground. Keep an eye out for the Snapping Dirt Clams. They'll pinch. And every once in a while a Dragon'll find a Dogger's hole and he'll breathe fire down it, hoping to char a meal. So watch when you see the light of holes or if you smell smoke."

"I will," Oyster said. He thought of Sister Patricia Tough-Pork who, when it was her turn to cook, burned the meat to blackened cubes that were impossible to chew. He didn't want to be someone's charred meal. Leatherbelly drew near to Oyster's heels. Oyster untied the map bag from his belt and was ready. "What do the Dragons look like?"

"Like Dragons, of course. Huge, green, lizardy creatures with enormous teeth," Drusser said.

The Growsel had to dig a slightly larger hole near the roots of a tree so that Oyster could fit; but once underground, the tunnels were wide and tall enough. Lanterns hung from the walls, casting a dim light. There were offshoots going in different directions, mazelike. Down some tunnels, all of the lanterns were yellow; down others, blue. Oyster couldn't tell what that meant.

Tipps, the Growsel, was quick. Oyster and Leatherbelly had to jog to keep up. The leather bag banged along behind. Soon enough, Oyster's lungs were burning in his chest. He took a moment to catch his breath. Leatherbelly paused and panted, too.

Oyster leaned against the tunnel wall. "Drusser!" he called ahead. "We need to rest!"

He heard Drusser say up ahead, though he couldn't see him, "Hurry up!"

Oyster gulped air. Then he heard a sudden flurry of clacking at his shoes and sharp pinches on his calves. He looked down, and his wet pants were covered with fat Snapping Clams.

Leatherbelly cried out. He had five attached to his tail. He wagged his tail violently and batted it against the tunnel wall. As soon as Oyster yanked the clams from his pants, they charged his face with their chattering shells. Oyster threw them back down the tunnel as fast as he could, but it didn't matter: more clams burrowed up from the dirt.

Oyster started running again. "C'mon, Leatherbelly!" he shouted. They had to keep moving.

They found Drusser up ahead. He held his finger to his lips. There was a cloud. "Smoke?" Oyster whispered. He was afraid of a Dragon.

Tipps was bucking nervously. Drusser was trying to keep steady. He shook his head. "Dirt," he said. "Being pawed up by eight legs."

"Eight legs?"

"Back up slowly," Drusser said. "The clams will start to sniff us out and they'll make a clatter."

Tipps and Oyster inched backward. Only Leatherbelly held his ground. His nostrils pulsing in the air, his fur up on his spine, he started to growl.

"Hush," said Oyster. "Back up, Leatherbelly."

But Leatherbelly only stiffened and bared his teeth. Oyster could see the Dirt Clams nosing up from the ground. He kept backing up. But Leatherbelly wouldn't follow suit.

"No," Drusser said, shaking his head vigorously. He was already headed back toward a split in the tunnels that they'd passed. "Spider Wolf isn't something to fight."

Oyster had heard of a wolf spider in the textbooks that Sister Mary Many Pockets used to teach him science—furry and eight-legged crawlers in a web—but what would a Spider *Wolf* look like? He didn't have to imagine for long. The cloud of dirt thinned, and the creature took shape. At first he looked just like an enormous dog, growling. He had a dark muzzle with large teeth, shiny eyes. It was the hunch of his back that made him different—that, and his eight legs. They were furry and long and double-jointed. They cocked out at the knees, and instead of a wolf's paws, the Spider Wolf had pincers, two of which were raised over its head like snakes ready to strike. The Dirt Clams were bouncing and snapping around Leatherbelly's paws. Oyster could feel his own heart skipping, but he tried to remain calm. He kept moving back slowly. "C'mon, Leatherbelly," he urged.

Leatherbelly wasn't ready to retreat. He lunged and barked loudly three times.

The Spider Wolf's eyes widened, and it hunched lower.

Leatherbelly shrank and gave a little apologetic bark more like clearing his throat. Too late. The Spider Wolf pawed at the ground.

"Run!" Drusser shouted.

They all turned and ran as fast as they could down one of the twisting tunnel's other passes. They turned and turned again. The Spider Wolf was gaining, and Oyster could hear its eight legs pounding against the dirt. He could hear its labored breath. They took one left turn after the next. Oyster felt dizzy.

"Keep up!" Drusser shouted.

"Are we going in circles?" Oyster cried back.

"Yes!" Drusser said. "It's working!"

Oyster wasn't sure what was working exactly. But he and Leatherbelly kept on turning down the same lantern-lit tunnels—yellow-lit tunnel; yellow-lit; then blue, blue, blue; and then yellow again—around and around. And the Spider Wolf began lagging behind. Oyster looked over his shoulder and saw the Spider Wolf bounce off a wall. It staggered in a dazed circle. Drusser had made it too dizzy to stand.

"Almost there!" Drusser cried. "Hurry!"

"Almost where?" Oyster shouted back.

Finally the tunnel seemed to come to a dead end. But as they reached it, Tipps hopped up and slid down a hole, disappearing from sight and taking Drusser with him.

Oyster and Leatherbelly ran to the hole, then stopped and looked down it.

"What are you waiting for?" Drusser called from below.

Oyster could hear the Spider Wolf coming. It was a distant moan. And the clams were already aware of their scent. Oyster could see the edges of their shells wriggling from the ground. He looked at Leatherbelly. "You first."

The dachshund pawed the ground but couldn't jump in.

"So *now* you've lost your nerve!" Oyster said. He jumped into the hole, which was really a winding slide that took him deeper underground.

He shot out of the bottom of the chute and landed on the floor. There was Drusser and Tipps, and sleeping on a hammock was a girl-Perth. She was small, as Perths tend to be. Not as small as Drusser, but still she seemed a miniature version of a human girl. She had brown hair, a perky nose, a jutting chin, and a few freckles spread out on her nose. Her bare feet were caked in dirt. She slept sprawled out with her hands behind her head. She was a cocky sleeper, Oyster was thinking. She looked like she was taking in the sun, but it was clear that she'd never taken in any sun. Her skin glowed so white, it nearly shone through the patches of dirt on her face.

Oyster sat there on the floor, just taking in the sight.

He didn't want to wake her. Even lying down, completely asleep, she looked poised for battle. But then Leatherbelly shot out of the chute and slammed into Oyster's back. The Spider Wolf, too big to fit down the hole, barked vigorously.

The girl jumped up, and in one swift motion, she grabbed a shovel and waved it in the air above her head. She glared at Oyster and Leatherbelly and swung the shovel backward, ready to flatten them right there. But Drusser jumped in between. "No, no!" he shouted. "He's good! Don't kill him! His parents were friends with your parents! He's the boy!"

"Don't kill me!" Oyster shouted. Leatherbelly jumped into his arms. Oyster closed his eyes tight and waited for the blow, but it didn't come. Slowly Oyster opened one eye and then the other. The girl was still holding the shovel over her head, but her face had gone still, her eyes wide and a little teary. She tilted her head. She looked at him in a way he recognized. Sister Mary Many Pockets had looked at him like this many times—and it was at these times that he could hear her heart speaking to his heart, a conversation leaping from one chest to the other. And, listening in this way that Oyster knew so well, without words, his heart could hear the girl's heart say, quite clearly: *The boy. I've been waiting for you.*

"Ippy?" Oyster said.

But then the voice of her heart went silent. She threw the shovel into a corner. She wiped her nose and rubbed her eyes as if they'd only gotten some dirt in them. "Yep. I'm Ippy. Sure. What's it to you?"

Chapter 14

Ippy, Underground

Ippy's room was spare. It didn't contain anything the least bit childlike. There were no textbooks, no bird's nests or eyedroppers or collections of moths in mesh boxes. There weren't any sentimental memorabilia like, say, a Dorsey's Pickled Foods box or a Royal Motel towel.

The walls were cool and mossy. The hammock was stretched between them. There was a bag of potatoes and turnips, a little cookstove with a pipe leading out of the room, and an overturned bucket. Drusser sat on it, resting one foot on his knee. He held on to one of Tipps' tusks like a staff.

"Found 'em hiding behind a tree," Drusser said. "But Oyster here crossed the Breathing River by swinging on vines."

"I've done that," Ippy snapped.

"And Leatherbelly here, he wrestled one of the Water Snakes and killed it."

"I've done that, too," Ippy said.

"And then underground, we met up with a Spider Wolf," Drusser said.

"Did you kill it?" Ippy asked.

"Well, no," Drusser said. "We just made it dizzy. They've got no balance."

"I know they've got no balance. But I'da killed it. One less Spider Wolf to deal with." She was still small, but she didn't *seem* small anymore. Oyster was afraid of her, weapon or not.

"Well," Drusser said. "I think they did fairly well for being new to the tunnels. It isn't easy."

"I know it isn't easy," Ippy said. "I've lived here all my life." She stared at Oyster. "Where have you been all these years?"

"I've been in a nunnery," Oyster said. "It's hard there, too."

"Spider Wolves? Dragons? Vicious Goggles? Snapping Dirt Clams?" At the mention of Spider Wolves, Oyster could hear the grunting breaths of the one they'd beaten to the hole. It was pawing and pacing above.

"No," Oyster said. "A lot of shushing and shooing. And, well, you can't really be a kid much in a nunnery. It isn't set up for it. In fact, I was the only kid there."

This information made Ippy stop. The Spider Wolf's bark was traveling away from the hole. It was a distant echo. She stared at Oyster. "You've been alone?"

"Well, no, there were the nuns."

"What are nuns?"

"They're mostly older women who all live together and wear black. These don't talk and they don't ever go out of the nunnery. I didn't go out except to get my tooth fixed, but it didn't get fixed, even."

"I've been alone too," Ippy said. "I don't go out aboveground much."

"So we've got that in common," Oyster said.

"We're strangers," Ippy said. "No matter what. I don't care if your parents knew mine." She sat down on the hammock. "How did you get here, anyway?"

Oyster felt shut off. Ippy was tougher than he'd expected. The Spider Wolf gave a howl overhead. "Through the Slippery Map," Oyster said, patting his leather bag.

Drusser and Ippy both sat up and leaned forward. She glanced at Drusser sharply.

"I didn't know," Drusser said. "I thought it was just his overnight bag!"

"Let's see it," Ippy said.

Oyster unbuckled the bag, showing her the large scroll.

"Pull it out," Ippy said.

"No," Oyster said, "I've got to keep it safe. I only want to take it out if I need to."

"Fine. You'll need it to get back one day," Ippy said. "You don't belong here."

"I might not want to go back," Oyster said. He was thinking about the nuns: Were they happy without him? Were they enjoying their peace and quiet for once?

"What do you want?" Ippy asked. "You want something from me. I can tell."

He cleared his throat. "I'm going to get my parents out of jail, defeat Dark Mouth, and save the Perths," he said.

Ippy started to laugh. Drusser did too. They laughed for a good long time, and Oyster simply patted Leatherbelly's ears and waited for them to stop.

"You're serious," Ippy said.

"I am serious," Oyster said. "And you're going to help me."

Drusser stood up nervously. "I've got to go," he said. "I've got things to do."

"Sit down," Ippy said, and Drusser did. "Look, Oyster." She leaned over him, pointing at his chest. "I don't help people. I survive on my own. I survive by my wits because I'm strong. My parents are dead. Your parents only got put in jail. You'll be fine. You got saved, right from the beginning. They got you out, and where have I been all this time? Hiding underground. I'm not helping anyone."

Oyster didn't mean to stand up, but he did. He felt hot, suddenly, all of his emotions rising to his face. He was unsteady on his feet. He said, "Your parents died. My parents sent me away. I don't know which one of us should be angrier!"

Ippy seemed surprised by Oyster's outburst. She sat back, a little stunned.

Oyster was surprised too. He looked at Drusser and Tipps, a little wide-eyed, wondering what might happen next, and then back at Ippy. He brushed off his cape, scratched his head through the top of his cap. Everyone was quiet. He had no choice. He was scared, but he had to go forward. He was needed. He looked at Leatherbelly and said, "Okay, then. We'll do it by ourselves." He stuck out his hand. "Nice to have met you."

Ippy paused, then stood. She came up only to Oyster's chest. She looked up at him and shook his hand.

"Best to climb back up the way we came?" Oyster asked.

"You won't get past the Spider Wolf. He's there waiting for you. You'll have to be patient," Ippy said.

Oyster didn't want to waste time. "Maybe not," he

said. He opened the leather bag and pulled out the menthol-flavored figs. He leaned into the chute, dug his shoes in as best he could, and started heading up.

"What are you doing?" Ippy asked nervously.

Oyster climbed until he saw the Spider Wolf's pincers, then he threw the paper bag upward. It landed on the lip of the chute. The Spider Wolf dug into the contents as Oyster eased himself back down.

"What was that?" Drusser asked.

"Some menthol-flavored figs," Oyster said. "They may make him listless and dull."

"I doubt it!" Ippy said.

But after a few minutes, the grunting and pawing were replaced by snores.

"Enough of them might even put it to sleep," Oyster said proudly, picking up his leather bag and walking to the mouth of the chute.

Ippy nodded. "Follow the blue-lit tunnels to Dark Mouth. Blue will take you to the other side."

"Thank you," Oyster said.

"If you even make it as far as Dark Mouth, he'll eat

you alive. But you won't make it," Ippy said. "I can tell."

Oyster pushed Leatherbelly ahead of him and up the chute. "I will make it, Ippy. You don't know anything about me. We're strangers, just like you said." Oyster's voice echoed in the chute. He imagined Dark Mouth's huge Torch, the smoke pouring into the sky, and his parents in prison somewhere beneath the Torch. "No," he said aloud. "I'm going to fix this." He followed Leatherbelly, who was dragging his calloused belly toward the dim light and the Spider Wolf snores above.

CHAPTER 15
MORE LAWLESS BEASTS

Oyster and Leatherbelly followed the blue-lit tunnels ever deeper underground.

Oyster didn't like being underground. It was cold and damp. Occasionally, he could hear Doggers through the tunnel walls, shouting, cursing, laughing. Sometimes they were singing angry fight songs. "Charge! Charge! Hoorah, hoorah!" He could also hear the whining claws of their Growsels. Sometimes they would wind up in a loud chorus—a pack of them, Oyster assumed, digging more tunnels.

Oyster was tired and hungry. He picked up the leather bag in his arms and unbuckled it while he kept walking so that he wouldn't get nipped at by Snapping Dirt Clams. Only the bag of non-menthol-flavored chocolate-covered figs was left now. Reaching into them, Oyster noticed a tremor in the Slippery Map. He stopped for a moment to see if he was the one causing it to shake. But the Slippery Map kept quaking. Oyster wasn't sure what to make of that. Ringet and Hopps had never mentioned anything like that. When he touched it, the Map popped up like it was kicked from within. Oyster was scared of it. He quickly cinched the bag of figs and buckled the leather bag and started rolling it again behind him.

"Keep an ear out for Spider Wolves," he told Leatherbelly, and they marched on, following blue-lit tunnels, chewing the chocolate-covered figs.

Without sunlight, it was hard to say how long they'd been walking. Hours had passed, Oyster knew that much. His legs were weak. He wanted to sit, just for a minute or two, but he didn't. The blue-lit tunnels were muddy now. Water trickled down the cool tunnel walls. Oyster was afraid of the walls collapsing. What then? They would be buried and no one would ever know.

It became too hard to pull the leather bag through the mud. The wheels got stuck. So Oyster picked it up once more and carried it. But this made it harder to ignore the Slippery Map shivering like it had a fever. What were Ringet and Hopps doing now? It had to be night. Their shift had to be over. Were they expecting to hear from him? Were they worried? Ringet seemed like a natural worrier.

"We don't need Ringet and Hopps's help," Oyster said to Leatherbelly. "But maybe we should just check in."

He opened the leather sack while walking. It was tricky, but they couldn't stop. The Snapping Dirt Clams would get them. He didn't unroll the Map. He exposed just the smallest sliver. He used the sharp edge of the bucket to make the smallest pinprick in the Map—just at Ringet's sink, just as he'd been instructed.

A thin plume of air escaped. "Hello!" he shouted; and just the thought of the two of them being out there, listening, this hope, pushed his emotions. He was wet and tired and homesick and lonesome and afraid and a bit lost. "Are you out there? Hello?"

The Map gave a hefty *thump* from somewhere on the other side.

Oyster rolled it up as quickly and tightly as he could, stooping for just a moment to shove it back in the bag.

That was it. That was all he got to say. He felt a little like crying. What he needed was a rest. What he needed was just a nice bit of luck, for something to go his way.

But the shaking had gotten worse. The leather bag bounced around in his arms. He felt like he wasn't holding the bag as much as wrestling it. It wasn't fair that he had to be in this mess to save his parents. *Shouldn't they be saving me?* Oyster thought. *Isn't that what parents do?* That's what Sister Mary Many Pockets had done all those years ago, picking a baby out of a box on a stoop and talking to him from her heart.

That's when he felt it again: a small voice in his heart. But this time it wasn't Sister Mary Many Pockets. He could have sworn it was Ippy, saying *Feel lucky, Oyster!* He looked around, but she was nowhere to be found. He said, "I'm sorry, Ippy. I am." He waited to feel her heart-voice again, but there was nothing. Did Ippy take apologies well? He doubted it.

His shoes were wet. The Map was kicking. Leatherbelly was whining. The Dirt Clams were clicking on the edges of the path. He trudged onward. Eventually the tunnel grew wider. Oyster followed as it opened into an underground meadow, and that's the moment things seemed to start to go his way.

It was beautiful. Oyster had never seen anything like it. The meadow was lit by a cluster of holes overhead. Weak sunlight slipped down. Plush and green and wide, the meadow was dotted with red ferns and an abundance of flowers that Oyster had never seen before: some with green stalks with buds like fat, pink baby fists; others with blue petals ringing a wet, black center; and, Oyster's favorite, a bush of red clustered berries pursed like lips. This bush reminded him of the nuns—their quiet mouths in the chapel tightened in wordless prayer.

Leatherbelly, exhausted, plopped down on a grassy patch. There was a bench, and Oyster figured that it would be safe to sit on it. Who would put a bench in a meadow if it attracted only Snapping Dirt Clams?

Oyster set down the leather bag with its kicking Map at his feet and sighed deeply. He was so tired. He quickly put his feet up on the bench and lay down. He was sure that he could smell the sun, and this was a great comfort. Leatherbelly kicked his feet out on the grass and closed his poppy eyes.

Oyster was nearly asleep when he heard whispering. He opened his eyes, and there were eyes staring back at him. The black, wet centers of the blue flowers faced him. They stared and blinked and stared like the cold, furious eyes of Mrs. Fishback. Oyster wasn't sure if he was seeing clearly. "Leatherbelly!" he said nervously.

Leatherbelly whined. He was pinned down by the pink baby fists of the flowers on the long green stalks. They had him by the scruff, his collar, his tail, and his paws. He let out a sad moan.

Oyster grabbed his leather bag and held it to his chest.

That's when the whispers rose up. "We don't like children!" they chimed. "Wouldn't it be awful if you disappeared!"

Oyster turned and saw the berries speaking to him. These weren't the lips of the nuns. No, these were menacing lips—speaking from Mrs. Fishback's mouth, a ring of lipstick. They hissed on, "A rotten boy! A stupid boy! Let's throw him out on his ear!" He hadn't been sure about the black eyes, but Mrs. Fishback's voice was unmistakable. Was his imagination influencing his parents' Imagined World? How was it possible? He didn't even have much of an imagination.

There was a loud *thud* overhead. The flowers trembled. The fists let go of Leatherbelly, and they all shrank away. There was another *thud* and another. "Footsteps," Oyster said. "Dragons!"

One of the sun holes grew dark. Oyster saw something

glassy, shimmering gray hovering above it. It was a living thing that darted until it spotted Oyster and held steady. And this is when Oyster knew it was an eye—a large gray eye gazing down on him. A Dragon's eye!

Oyster grabbed Leatherbelly and the bag and ran. The eye disappeared and a flame shot into the meadow. And then another sun hole darkened. Another eye, this one closer. Again they ran. There were more footsteps overhead, more Dragons. A herd of Dragons? Was that possible? Did they travel in herds? Now all of the holes were filled with either eyes or fire.

Oyster tried to find the tunnel that had led them here, but the ferns and flowers were so thick and high, he couldn't. The berries were singing, "Rotten boy! Stupid boy!" And the pink baby fists had grown bigger, fatter, and thicker, with tough knuckles and nails—like Mrs. Fishback's hands, he was sure of it. They snatched at Oyster and Leatherbelly and tried to hold them. Oyster pulled back one gnarled finger and then another until the hand popped loose. He stood up, clutched Leatherbelly tight, and kicked at the fists, finally yanking him free.

They dodged one shot of fire after another. Oyster got on his knees and pulled Leatherbelly into a bed of flowers to hide, but the flowers bowed away to reveal them.

The gray eyes were always there, the fire next. It was

dark now and smoky. The only light came from the blasts of fire like lightning bolts. Oyster and Leatherbelly ran to the meadow's edge, looking for an exit, but there was none. Oyster patted the dirt wall frantically.

The Dragons drew closer. The cavern was hot and filled with smoke—it caught in their lungs and made it almost impossible to breathe. Oyster's eyes were watering so badly he could barely see. Soon he was on his knees, coughing, gripping the bag tightly. He looked up and saw the gray eye of a Dragon staring straight down at him. He thought, *This is it.* Holding the leather bag with one arm and Leatherbelly with the other, he gave one last sharp roll to the right.

The ground collapsed beneath them and they fell.

Eventually they landed hard in a pit. Oyster could see only the dim shapes of a cluster of Goggles—but these Goggles had pointy yellow teeth and dense fur. His head was ringing. "Ippy?" he said. "Ippy, help!"

There was a high laugh and then a smile appeared—a large, glittery smile like that on Dr. Fromler's billboard—and then, before Oyster passed out, he heard: "Charming! The boy! Finally! At last!"

CHAPTER 16

THE WEST COAST OF BONELAND

When Oyster jolted awake, he was sweaty. When had he fallen asleep? A pair of Vicious Goggles snarled on either side of him, and this alerted a Perth in a nearby lounge chair. The Perth was wearing swim trunks, a foil sun-reflector on his chest, and a pair of blue sunglasses. He looked freshly broiled. Oyster found himself in a lounge chair too, poolside. The morning sun was pouring down.

Oyster remembered a night of drifting in and out of consciousness. He knew he'd been transported in the dark over rough terrain. Occasionally he'd felt the knock of what seemed like a wheel hitting a rut, but then he would fade into dreams that he couldn't remember.

"He's up!" the Perth said. "The boy's up! Lovely!" He looked familiar to Oyster, but Oyster couldn't place him. He smelled strong, a little like the wood polish used in the nunnery but fruitier. The Perth lifted his glass, empty except for a chewed lime. "Refresher!" he said, clapping his hands. "Refresher!"

An elderly Perth, quite stooped, wearing a black suit, hopped out from a gazebo. He was carrying a silver pitcher on a tray. "Here you are, sir," the old Perth said, filling the glass.

"It's the boy, Fraca," the tan Perth said. "See him!" He pointed at Oyster.

"I do, sir," Fraca replied.

"We're so pleased!" the tan Perth said. "You'll find we're very civilized here—even to the enemy. Aren't we, Fraca?"

"We are," Fraca said.

Oyster was the enemy? Where were Leatherbelly and the Slippery Map? He reached up and patted the necklace with the silver bucket. It was still there, hidden under his T-shirt. A relief.

He studied the Perth now. There was something familiar about his eyebrows. When he sipped his drink, they drew up in the middle with swelling emotion—as if his eyebrows belonged on the face of someone singing his heart out. And then the Perth pressed his hand to his pink chest and said, "I'm your host." And in that moment Oyster knew exactly who he was. In unison, Oyster and the Perth said, "Vince Vance."

And just as in the show, an unseen band kicked up.

"You know me?" Vince Vance shouted over the music. "I'm flattered!" But it was clear that Vince Vance fully expected everyone to know exactly who he was.

Oyster also knew where he was: the West Coast of Boneland. It was the spot that Ringet had told Hopps to include on his makeshift map while trying to plot Oyster's course to Dark Mouth. But Hopps had refused, saying there was no need, that Oyster wasn't going to be taking the time to sun himself by a pool. Oyster would have liked to have seen this spot on the map now, to have his bearings. He knew that he was in the west, on a coast, but how far from Dark Mouth?

He tried to look around casually for Leatherbelly and the Slippery Map. He couldn't see either. The Vicious Goggles didn't like his curiosity. They growled again.

"Hush, boys!" Vince Vance said. The music had died down. "Hush now, sweeties." Vince Vance patted one of the Vicious Goggles on the head, then turned to Oyster. "Is it that you're looking for your pudgy little friend? And a certain personal item?"

"Yes," Oyster said. "Where are they?"

Vince Vance said, "We'd like to make you an offer. This doesn't have to be messy."

"Who is 'we'?" Oyster asked.

"Oh, well, I work for Dark Mouth. I'm a spokesperson!"

Here he smiled brilliantly, and Oyster recalled Dr. Fromler's glittery smile. "You, too, Oyster R. Motel, can have the good life I lead, that Dark Mouth has given me!" He spread his arms open wide, showing the sparkling pool water, the elderly butler, the enormous mansion. "Those Perths may have filled your head with nostalgic notions of things like . . . petals drifting down from giant flowers. That sort of business. Did they?"

Oyster remembered Ringet telling him about the twenty-foot flowers that had once sat where the Torch was now, the petals covering the valley. He'd liked the sound of it. The flowers had been turned to bone. Oyster nodded.

"There are better things than giant flower petals, Oyster." Vince Vance clapped his hands, and Fraca appeared again. This time he was pushing a plush stroller on oversized wheels. The stroller was smothered in white frills and ribbon trim. Fraca pushed it to Oyster. Inside was Leatherbelly, freshly groomed. He smelled like peaches. His hair was blown into a pomp. He was lazily nibbling on a jerky strip.

"Leatherbelly!" Oyster said. "What happened?"

Leatherbelly smiled. His tail wagged joyfully, like a little bell ringing on his back side.

"The beast is content," Vince Vance explained. "He's living the good life. Wouldn't you like to live the good life?"

"I don't think so," Oyster said, staring out across the pool. "I've got work to do."

"Dark Mouth knows the work you're trying to get done. Your parents, blah, blah, saving the Perths, blah, blah. Defeating Dark Mouth, blah, blah. You haven't been very kind, deciding to defeat someone you don't know one factual thing about!" Oyster felt a little bad about this.

"Listen, the Perths are using you. And, you see, Dark Mouth," Vince Vance went on, "he just wants you to enjoy life, Oyster! There's so much to enjoy. You need a tour!"

Vince Vance was trying to catch Oyster's eye, but Oyster kept his eyes on two large mahogany doors that seemed to lead into a tall mansion. The Perths weren't using him. They needed him. But Vince Vance clapped his hands again. "Inside! Inside!"

Two more elderly, stooped Perths filed out of the gazebo. Fraca pushed Leatherbelly in his floofy stroller, and the others tipped back the lounge chairs, which happened to be on wheels, and rolled Oyster and Vince Vance around the pool toward the mahogany doors. "Faster!" Vince Vance cried. "Faster!"

The mansion was gigantic, and the elderly Perths pushed the lounge chairs at such a fast clip across the marble floors that a wind kicked up. Vince Vance leaned into it. The foil sun-reflector spun around to his back and flapped.

They whizzed into the music room, where the band was waiting for its cues. The musicians wore bow ties and pasty smiles. "I'm your host! Vince Vance!" he shouted, and the band revved up. "You can have your own theme song!" Vince shouted over the music. He listened with his eyes closed, his eyebrows hitched up; and then when the song was done, he said, "Go on, Oyster. Give it a try. Just like I did. They'll make one just for you on the spot!"

"Really?" Oyster asked.

"Of course!"

Oyster felt a little shy. He cleared his throat. Leatherbelly sat up in his stroller.

"Nice and loud now!"

"Okay," Oyster said, and then he shouted, "I'm your host! Oyster R. Motel!" And a new song kicked up, a great, big tune with full horns. It suited Oyster, or some version of him that he'd like to be—a big, loud, famous version.

The song ended.

Vince Vance clapped his hands. "On we go! Faster now!" he said. "Let's eat!"

The elderly Perths tore down a hallway, then banged through two swinging doors into a kitchen thrumming with chefs. The room was billowing with scented steam in a sea of puffed white hats. Vince Vance was singing out, "Sautéed Snapping Dirt Clams! Poached Spider Wolf eggs stuffed with buttered creamy fat! Fried Dragon dipped in marmalade!" As they whizzed past, Vince Vance held open his mouth. The chefs popped bits into it.

"Open up!" Vince Vance shouted.

Leatherbelly nipped the food from the chefs' hands before they even had time to give it to him. Oyster didn't open his mouth just yet. He liked the sound of mar- malade and buttered creamy fat, but Spider Wolf eggs, fried Dragon? Still, he was extremely hungry and very tired of figs, chocolate-covered or not. Everything smelled delicious. He closed his eyes and opened his mouth. It was filled up with flavors he'd never tasted before: mixes of sweets and sours, gummy and melting and crunchy. He loved them all.

"Here we eat well! No restrictions like those lowly Perths in Boneland. No digging for roots like the Doggers. Faster now! Onward!"

"Thank you," Oyster called out. "Thanks!" Why hadn't Ippy found this place? He thought back to her little damp home at the bottom of a chute. Did she even know that this existed? And that's when he remembered calling to her for help after landing hard on his back and every- thing going dim. Had she been listening then? Was she still refusing to help him? Well, he didn't need her help.

The chefs bowed, tipping their poofy hats.

The elderly Perths flew down another hallway, full speed. Oyster could hear them panting. He felt guilty about how hard they were working. He said, "I can walk. I don't mind."

"Don't be absurd!" Vince Vance said. Then he whispered loudly, as if the Perths couldn't hear. "What else would they do if not this!"

Well, maybe that is true, Oyster thought. *I mean, better here than at Orwise Suspar's Refinery, sucking powder into their lungs.* Plus, Oyster liked the wind in his hair. He liked leaning into the breeze like Vince Vance.

Vince Vance shouted, "Note the gold trim!" He pointed to ceilings and chair rails and banisters. "Note the statues!"

Oyster stared at the statues, posed in a little hunting scene. They were white, like bone: a Dogger holding a quiver; two Perths poised with their arrows, the bows' strings held tight to their faces.

"Toys!" Vince Vance ordered.

The elderly Perths turned left and sprinted.

The toy room was glorious and massive. The elderly Perths slowed down so Oyster could take it all in. Windup Dragons lumbered through high plastic grass. The ceiling buzzed with large, fake black birds with bright red beaks (Blood-Beaked Vultures?) and Iglits. Vince Vance pushed a button and the berry bushes sang the "Home Sweet Home" song. The baby fists snapped their fingers and the blue-petaled flowers swayed.

"Try the slide," Vince Vance said.

Oyster got out of the lounge chair and climbed the stairs built into the leg of a huge plastic Dragon. Vince Vance pushed a button and the Dragon's tail began to wag. Oyster slipped down it, swaying this way and that. He'd never seen anything like this. A place just for children! He hadn't even been allowed to sit on the merry-go-round horse with the shiny smile in Dr. Fromler's office.

"Do you like it?" Vince Vance shouted.

"I love it!"

Vince Vance smiled and nodded. "Dark Mouth is very thoughtful, Oyster. He had this designed for you!"

Oyster felt like crying. No one had ever made so much for him—just for him! His whole life, up until this point, was geared around other people's needs: the importance of orthopedic nun shoes, cushions on the kneelers, more bran in breakfast foods.

"There's more!" Vince Vance said. He pointed to a window, and when Oyster looked out of it, he saw a boy holding a blue umbrella. The boy wasn't wearing the leg braces. He didn't really look anything like the boy at the Dragon Palace, but he was dancing and singing, "Come play, Oyster! Come on and play!"

"Is he real?" Oyster asked.

"It's all as real as you want it to be!"

Oyster stared down at the boy. He waved, and the

boy picked up a blue umbrella and spun it over his head as he danced.

"How did you know?" Oyster asked.

"We have ears in every wall. Eyes in every sliver of light. Dark Mouth is attentive. He's watching over you!"

Oyster thought back. He had mentioned the boy with the blue umbrella when he was at Ringet's house. Had someone been watching him there? Did they know everything? The whole plan? Was the plan doomed to fail?

"We'd like you to stay here, Oyster. Dark Mouth wants you to be as happy as I am. I'm happy, aren't I, Fraca?"

"Yes, sir," Fraca said.

"We need only one thing," Vince Vance said. "Come with me. I'll explain."

Oyster looked down at the boy on the street below. He wanted to tell him that he'd be back soon, but there wasn't time. Vince Vance clapped his hands again. "To the sky room."

Oyster jumped into the chair and was whisked away. At the end of a very long hall, they came to a room with a door in each of the four walls. The room was empty except for a table, and on top of the table was the leather bag—now wriggling and jerking madly.

Oyster was afraid of the Slippery Map. He was pretty sure that he wouldn't mind staying here with Vince Vance for a while; but the Map, now violently skidding around the tabletop, was a reminder of his old prom-ises. Ringet and Hopps—he hadn't been thinking about them at all. *Were* they using him, dangling the promise of his parents in front of him so that he would defeat Dark Mouth for them? What did he know about them, really? Nothing except that they were willing to let him get eaten by a Spider Wolf and charred by a Dragon. Dark Mouth only wanted Oyster to enjoy the good life!

The elderly Perths—exhausted, breathless—parked Vince Vance, Oyster, and Leatherbelly in the middle of the room. They reclined the lounge chairs until Vince Vance and Oyster were lying flat. The ceiling was made of pink tinted glass, so the sky appeared to be filled with rosy clouds.

"What we need," Vince Vance said, "is a lesson on how to use the Slippery Map. It's been an item that Dark Mouth has been interested in for some time. But he's never had the opportunity to be in its presence before. I believe one of the reasons he's become so attached to your parents has been the hope that the Map would somehow find them. And in a sense, it has come looking, hasn't it?"

"Dark Mouth is *attached* to my parents? I thought he had them in prison!"

Vince Vance laughed, trilling and high. "Jail? Silliness. Perth-talk! They can't believe that your parents could be so happy away from them. Of course your parents don't want to go back to that dreadful place. Well, now that you've been here, you can imagine that they aren't so bad off, are they?"

"Oh," Oyster said. Yes, he could imagine. But this didn't sit quite right with him. Why wouldn't they come to find him? I mean, it was one thing to be in jail but another to be enjoying a plush life of luxury and choosing to stay put.

"The Perths have probably told you that Dark Mouth wants to use the Map so that he can take over the other side. Haven't they?"

Oyster nodded.

"Pure nonsense! Dark Mouth is actually devoted to reaching out to as many people as possible." Vince Vance continued, "He's limited here in what he can do for the community. And he'd really like to branch out, network, perhaps do some partnering on the other side of the Gulf of Wind and Darkness. As would I! I'd be marvelous on the other side, you know. I have a real desire to do some *real* acting! Do you understand?"

"I think so," Oyster said. "Dark Mouth is interested in community service." Every Christmas season at the nunnery, Sister Helen Quick Fingers would have all of the nuns crochet dolls for the poor. She'd make it a contest and always won every year.

"Yes! Community service! Nicely put!" Vince Vance said.

"And you want to be famous." Sister Elouise of the Occasional Cigarette liked to put on a small Christmas pageant every year. Oyster had outgrown playing the baby Jesus and had been demoted to a mule. "Like in Hollywood."

"Hollywood?" Vince Vance liked the sound of this word. "What is Hollywood?"

"It's a place on the other side. I've never been, but it's for people like you, who want to be famous."

"I like it!" Vince Vance said dreamily. "I like it very much!"

They continued to stare at the pink sky. "Get out the Map, would you, Fraca?"

Oyster could hear Fraca unbuckling the bag, but the sky was moving slowly and the view made Oyster so relaxed that he wasn't worrying much about the Map. He watched the limb of a tall tree that curved over the glass roof. It dipped in the breeze.

"Hypnotic, those clouds, aren't they?" Vince Vance said. "You like it here, don't you?"

Oyster nodded.

"You are such a kind boy, Oyster. Very generous. That's what we like about you so much. You're always willing to help someone in need!"

"I try," Oyster said, sitting up. Fraca had already unrolled the Map in both directions, revealing the Gulf of Wind and Darkness, a bit of Baltimore on one side and Boneland on the other. But the Map wasn't sitting on the ground flat. It was jittering and jumping. Vince Vance was standing over it. "Is it always like this?" He was still wearing his swim trunks, the sun-reflector flat on his back. The blue sunglasses were pushed up on top of his head.

"No," Oyster said.

Vince Vance was a little afraid of the Map. He was skittish. "Well, let's just get on with it. How do we travel through?" he asked.

"It's pretty easy, really," Oyster said. He lifted the necklace over his head. He knelt at the edge of the Map. It was jerking off of the ground, making it hard to find a good spot to open it up. But Oyster flattened it out with his hand, and then he took the edge of the silver bucket. He scratched at a spot, and the Map quickly burst open so hard that the sheer force bowled Oyster over flat on his back.

He sat up and saw that it wasn't gusty wind and darkness. It was black clothes and a flapping veil, and the round face and body of Sister Mary Many Pockets. She popped out of the Map with such force that she flew into the air and landed a dozen feet away. Then the Map stopped shaking and sealed up tightly.

Vince Vance gasped. "What is this?"

Sister Mary Many Pockets scrambled toward Oyster and hugged him. Oyster was confused. She was here. She'd come through the Map somehow to find him. He could hear her joyous heart: *I've found you! I've found you!*

Oyster was confused. "You came for me?" he asked.

She nodded and rubbed his head. *Of course I came for you, Oyster,* her heart cried out. *You are my boy!*

Sister Mary Many Pockets truly loved him. His eyes filled with tears. He felt choked with emotion. How could he have doubted her? It was so plain to him now. She'd always loved him. She always would. She'd fought her way to him. She didn't want a quiet life of peace, and Oyster didn't want the good life as offered by Vince Vance. *Yes,* his heart said back, *I am your boy!*

He looked around the sky room. But what had he done? He'd given up the secret of the Map. He'd given into glitter and promises—just what the Mapkeeper had warned him about!

Vince Vance glared at Oyster and Sister Mary Many Pockets and the now calm Slippery Map. His tan face had turned ruddy. He was furious. "Are you trying to trick us, Oyster R. Motel? Have you brought us a fake? A bad replica that only spits out old women?"

Sister Mary Many Pockets stiffened. She didn't like the description. Leatherbelly was sitting up in his stroller now, and the elderly Perths, terrified, had backed away to the corners of the sky room.

"Yes!" Oyster said. "That's what I've done!" He stood up. "This map is a fake!"

Vince Vance glared at Oyster. "You," he said, "cannot be trusted!" He bundled up the Map in his arms. "Dark Mouth will be collecting all maps, slippery or not!" He then clapped his hands violently over his head, and in an instant, the room filled with Vicious Goggles.

"Take her away to the Blood-Beaked Vultures!" he said to the Vicious Goggles.

"No!" Oyster cried out. He and Sister Mary Many Pockets held on to each as tightly as they could. But the Goggles dragged Sister Mary Many Pockets and Oyster apart.

Oyster! her heart was crying out. *Oyster, I will find you again! I will!*

She disappeared through a side door, leaving Oyster and Leatherbelly alone with Vince Vance and the rest of the Vicious Goggles.

"You're done for, Oyster. It's over for you and your beast." Leatherbelly whimpered. Vince Vance glanced at the Vicious Goggles. "Why don't you all enjoy these two as your evening snack, my sweeties? It would bring me great pleasure to watch, Oyster. But as you know, we try to be quite civilized here. And I would like to offer you privacy in your death."

Oyster stood there, shaking his head. "But you wanted me to live here! What about the boy with the blue umbrella? He was real, wasn't he?"

Vince Vance laughed. "Oh, Oyster! Of course not!"

He sat down on his lounge chair, letting his sun-glasses plop to his nose. "Fraca!" he shouted.

Fraca appeared from the shadows, glancing at Oyster with an expression of deep despair, and rolled Vince Vance from the room.

Oyster ran to Leatherbelly and scooped him up in his arms. There was nothing to do, really. They were stuck. It was over for them. Sister Mary Many Pockets had been taken away. The Map was gone. And it was Oyster's fault. He'd failed. But this seemed right, in a way. He'd been drawn in by glitter. They'd played on his weaknesses. And yet he felt better knowing that his parents weren't living it up with Dark Mouth. He felt better thinking that they didn't want to be here but were being held against their will. (The gnawing questions he hadn't been able to ask were still there: Did they miss him? Did they regret these years without him? Did they, could they, love him?)

The Vicious Goggles inched closer, drooling and

sniffing and snapping. Oyster looked up one last time at the pink sky. It was beautiful. He looked up at it and was simply thankful for it, thankful in general. He'd been lucky, really. Sister Mary Many Pockets loved him.

Just when he could feel the Vicious Goggles' breath in his face, he heard a soft thud from above. Two dirty bare feet appeared on the glass, and then a face, a face made pink by the tinted glass, a face dotted with freckles and smeared with dirt. Ippy!

I'm here! her heart said.

And then with a loud *bang*, one of the far doors opened. And there, holding their bows and arrows, were three of the statues, powdery white but not statues at all: Drusser, Ringet, and Hopps.

CHAPTER 17

THE BATTLE OF TONGUES AND ARROWS

Drusser, Ringet, and Hopps were covered in a clumpy white paste made of powdered sugar, Oyster figured, from Orwise Suspar and Sons Refinery. Ringet and Hopps were still in their uniforms. Drusser looked like a small ghost. With each bold step toward the Goggles, a white, dusty cloud plumed around them.

The Goggles lumbered slowly forward with hunched backs. They didn't hop like frogs. Their claws clacked against the gleaming wood floor, the webs between them shining.

"You okay, Oyster?" Hopps called out. "Under the circumstances?"

"Well, not exactly," Oyster said, petting Leatherbelly. He didn't want to tell them all that had gone wrong, but knew he had to. "Sister Mary Many Pockets has been hauled off to be eaten by vultures. And the Slippery Map is gone. Vince Vance is taking it to Dark Mouth. And, well, I don't like Goggles. Be careful."

"Sister Mary who?" Drusser asked.

"Not the Blood-Beaked Vultures!" Ringet screeched.

"The Slippery Map is gone?" Hopps said. "Gone?"

"Yes," Oyster said. "I'm sorry! It was all my fault!"

The Goggles were closing in. "We can discuss this later," Hopps said to Oyster. He took aim at the largest Goggle. "I can shoot you right between the eyes, Goggle. Why don't you call off the troops?"

"We'll take you all out!" Drusser said. "Don't tempt us!"

"I thought we weren't going to kill anything!" Ringet said. "You promised, Hopps!" He was aiming at one Goggle and then the next and the next, wildly, as if to prove that they were outnumbered.

"Be quiet, Ringet," Hopps said.

Just then a Goggle shot out his tongue and snatched Ringet's cap off his head, swallowing it as though it were a fly. Ringet screamed.

"Stop it, Ringet!" Hopps yelled. "Shape up!"

Oyster heard a noise overhead. He looked up and saw Ippy, using a chisel and hammer to poke holes through the rose-tinted glass, creating a perforated circle. Her small, muscular arms worked efficiently, carving out a large circle in the skylight. Bits of glass tumbled down, raining on a few warty Goggle backs. Oyster, holding Leatherbelly, backed away. He felt helpless unarmed.

The largest Goggle leaped at Hopps, snagging his arm, ripping his sleeve. Another Goggle smacked Drusser's shoulder with his tongue. Drusser toppled backward, then rolled to his feet and shot an arrow at the Goggle attacking Hopps. The arrow hit the Goggle's webbing, pinning a claw to the ground. Ringet limped to hide behind a pillar. He tried to aim, but his arrow rattled against its bow.

And then the battle began in earnest: pink tongues flying everywhere, sharp teeth, lunging beasts, and arrows flying at webbed feet. Just when Oyster thought they were doomed, Ippy broke through the hole she'd made, and a big pane of glass shattered on the floor. She dropped down a rope tethered to something out of sight.

"Go!" Hopps yelled from a window ledge where he was taking aim at the Goggles' feet. "Oyster, you first."

Oyster ran to the rope, scooping up Leatherbelly and shoving him down his shirtfront so he could use both arms to pull himself up. The rope burned his palms. The violent scene below him seemed to sway. He felt dizzy. When Oyster got to the top, Ippy was leaning over the hole with her hand out. Oyster grabbed it.

"I thought you didn't help people," Oyster said.

"Well, it's a strange thing," Ippy said. "I mean, I've never felt anything like it, but, well, I knew you were in trouble. I heard you call out for help. It's like a voice in my— I can't explain it."

"Your heart feels like it's talking to my heart sometimes?"

She looked at Oyster. "Yeah," she said. "Why is that?"

"I think it might mean we're friends," Oyster said.

Ippy didn't want to smile. She tried not to. But the smile showed up anyway, popping open on her face. Oyster smiled too.

"Ringet, go! Your turn!" Hopps yelled below.

Oyster and Ippy leaned over to watch.

"I can't!" Ringet cried from behind the pillar. The air was still loud with the snap of tongues and moaning.

"Go!" Hopps yelled. Oyster noticed that Hopps was hurt. The rip in his shirt was soaked with blood.

"C'mon, Ringet!" Drusser shouted, letting an arrow fly.

Ringet zigzagged around the Goggles, both arms protecting his head. He dodged their furious tongues, grabbed onto the rope, and shinnied up, with his one leg stiff and helpless. Oyster and Ippy helped hoist him to the roof. He lay breathless on his back. "I'm afraid of heights. I can't look down!"

"Drusser, go!" Hopps yelled.

Drusser was being chased by a wild Goggle with warts

the size of horns. Some of the tongues smacking him were stickier than others; and because Drusser was so small, the tongues dragged him in toward each mouth before he found the strength to pull free. Hopps took aim at the warty Goggle, but it was quick and dodged the arrows with erratic leaps. Finally, as Drusser ran and jumped for the rope Hopps nailed the warty Goggle to the floor.

The last few loose Goggles, heavily furred and leap-ing, cornered Hopps on the win-dowsill.

Drusser was half-way up the rope. He shouted to Oyster and Ippy, "Help me swing the rope out to Hopps."

Ippy and Oyster reached down, grabbed the rope, and pulled it back and forth so that it swung Drusser like a pendulum. The end of the rope whipped closer and closer to Hopps. Finally, it was close enough for him to grab. He jumped and rode through the barrage of tongues. He tried to climb, but his wounded shoulder was of no use. "I can't," he said. "Just go on. Go on without me!"

"He's bleeding," Drusser said, climbing onto the roof.

Ringet rolled to his stomach and saw the bloody arm for the first time. "He's hurt! It's my fault!" Ringet cried. "I could have helped him and I didn't! I'm worthless at all of this. I'm a coward!"

"C'mon," Oyster said. "Let's haul him up!" Ippy, Drusser, and Leatherbelly grabbed the rope. And after crawling unevenly across the glass, Ringet joined in, too. Hand over hand, they tugged until Hopps emerged through the hole. The Goggles' howls echoed below so loudly that the glass roof shook.

"How did you know I needed you?" Oyster asked as they crawled across the roof to the branches.

"We got your message through the Map," Hopps said, wincing through the pain in his arm. "It was cut short but sounded urgent."

"We met up with Ippy and Drusser along the way," Ringet said. "Ippy had heard a message too. She helped us onto the back of some delivery trucks, in past the Goggles. It was my idea to play statues," he added proudly.

"We don't have much time now," Ippy said. She was already on a branch, climbing down. "Someone's waiting for us."

"I've got to save Sister Mary Many Pockets," Oyster said. "She's going to be fed to the Vultures." He couldn't bear to call them "Blood-Beaked."

"Oh, dear," Ringet said, staring up at the sky. "Oh, help me, help me, help me."

"I know someone who will help with your Sister Mary Many Pockets," Ippy said.

"Who's this?" Hopps said suspiciously.

"Yes, who, Ippy?" Drusser asked.

They were all on the tree now, using the branches as a ladder to the ground. The underbrush was dense and the trees were knit together with vines. Oyster could hear birds and distant hissing and other noises he didn't recognize. It made him nervous.

"Eshma Weegrit," Ippy said.

"Eshma Weegrit?" Ringet whispered in a reverent tone. "I've wanted to meet her all my life."

"Who's Eshma Weegrit?" Oyster asked.

"Don't get your hopes up, Ringet," Hopps said, inspecting his gash. "She can't still be alive."

"She is still alive," Ippy said.

"Then why hasn't she helped the Cause? With her powers, she could do wonders for us." Hopps sounded bitter.

"She's a guru," Ippy said.

"And gurus don't have to help the Cause?" Hopps shot back.

"*The* Eshma Weegrit?" Drusser asked. "Are you sure?"

"Are there a lot of Eshma Weegrits?" Ippy asked. She took out a large knife and started to cut through the underbrush, making a trail.

"Who's Eshma Weegrit?" Oyster asked again, following her.

"She can cure your arm, Hopps," Ringet said. "And, well, she can cure my locked leg, too. She can! I've always heard it said." Oyster wanted to believe this was true. He thought of the boy at the Dragon Palace with the leg braces. Could Eshma Weegrit cure him, too? But this thought filled Oyster's chest with the tight sadness of being homesick. Without the Slippery Map, Oyster wondered if he'd ever see the boy again.

"We're not meeting up with Eshma Weegrit. She doesn't exist," Hopps said. "We're just going to try to make it through the valley alive, and if we do, we'll be lucky."

"She does so!" Ippy said.

Oyster was frustrated, tired of being ignored. If someone was going to help Sister Mary Many Pockets, then he wanted to know something about her. "Who is Eshma Weegrit?" he shouted.

"Never mind that just now," Drusser said. "First we've got to get out of this forest."

"Who's stopping us?" Oyster asked.

"Not who, *what*," Drusser said.

CHAPTER 18

INFESTATIONS, ATTACKS BY AIR, AND ANCIENT FIRE-BREATHERS

Ringet started reading the highlighted passages from a worn paperback, *How to Handle Lawless Beasts*. Oyster assumed it was one of the outlawed books he kept in his oversized soup cans.

" 'Chapter One, Infestations,' " Ringet blurted quickly. " 'Flying Three-Horned Rhinoceros-Ants, Jelly Roaches, Killer One-Eyed Slugs.' "

"Jelly Roaches might taste good spread on a mushroom, but they're poisonous," Ippy said, chopping vines. "Your tongue will swell up."

Oyster kept an eye on the ground. Jelly Roaches seemed like something that would crawl slowly and appear without you knowing it.

"It gets worse!" Ringet said.

"Please stop," Hopps said. He was holding his arm close to his side.

"'Chapter Two,'" Ringet went on, "'Attacks by Air: Treehogs, Blue Bats, Dart-Spitting Winged Snakes.'"

"I was once struck in the head by a Dart Spitter," Drusser said. "I couldn't think straight for a week."

Oyster's eyes searched in every direction: above for Blue Bats, below for Killer One-Eyed Slugs. "Dragons?" Oyster asked. He didn't like Dragons. "Are they in there?"

"A whole chapter on Dragons alone. 'Ancient Fire-Breathers.'" Ringet started flipping to the chapter.

"Put the book away," Hopps growled. "It's too late. Don't you see that?"

Ringet shoved the book in his pocket and ran to Hopps at the end of the line. He grabbed his good arm and helped prop up Hopps with his shoulder. "It's my fault you're hurt, Hopps. The least I can do is be prepared so it doesn't happen again!" Ringet looked up and pointed. "Treehog!"

Oyster stared at the spot. He was relieved to see that it was just a lump on the side of a tree, and he was about to say so; but the lump twisted and a snout and two beady eyes emerged. Oyster picked up his pace and got closer to Ippy. Drusser was beside her now, helping cut the trail. They both stopped so abruptly that Oyster rammed into them.

"What is it?" Hopps and Ringet asked.

"Charred clearing," Drusser said.

"And smoked turtle shells, finely picked," Ippy added.

Oyster was on his feet, looking over her shoulder at a pile of fifty shells on the ground.

They sat on a parched spot of bare ground ringed by fried trees. "What does it mean?" he asked.

"Dragon Perths," Hopps said. "My family comes from Dragon Perths way back."

"Dragon Perths?" Ringet said, pulling out his book again.

"They won't be in your book! They're not beasts," Hopps said defensively.

"They work with the Dragons," Ippy explained. "The Dragon cooked the turtles and the Dragon Perths picked them clean, sharing with the Dragon."

"It's a delicate friendship, though," Drusser said. "Sometimes a Dragon Perth gets swallowed up."

Ippy reached down and touched the shells. "Still warm," she said. "They could be anywhere."

"Maybe the Dragon Perths can help!" Ringet said. "I mean, if they're your kind, Hopps, maybe they'd be on our side."

"Or feed us to the Dragon," Hopps said.

Everyone was looking around, turning in slow circles.

Oyster stared at a shrub with yellow berries. One of the berries winked and a pale eye exposed itself. "There!" Oyster said.

"Get down!" Hopps yelled.

They all dived to the ground.

Oyster found himself squeezed in next to Ippy. "This isn't good," he said.

"You'll be okay, Oyster," she said, looking up at him. "You're tough."

"You think so?" he asked.

Ippy nodded.

Oyster couldn't help but smile—even though they were in a bad spot. Ippy thought he was tough! Imagine that! Things swished past overhead. He wanted to know what they were, so he took a quick look and then wished he hadn't. Balls covered in long needles.

"Spike Balls," Drusser said. "They'll knock you out. Stay low."

Oyster saw a Spike Ball land in the smoky clearing. It unfurled. Four legs appeared. *A porcupine,* Oyster thought, except that it had long, gapped front teeth and wore an unpleasant sneer.

"This is bad," Ringet said with his eyes closed tight.

"We're targets now," Ippy said. "If we stay crouched, it's just a matter of time before the animals start to hunt us down."

Oyster knew that Ippy was right. He thought of the Snapping Dirt Clams that burrowed up from underground.

The Blue Bats were the first to start hovering overhead. Shortly after that, Oyster spotted the blunt head
of a snake. *Don't fly!* Oyster said to himself. *Please don't
fly.* He scooted down as best as he could into a ball, like
the porcupines. But then he saw the Jelly Roaches. A
small, shiny line of them moving toward his shoes.

"We've got to make this stop," Ippy said.

"Or we're doomed," Drusser added.

"Doomed!" Ringet said, grabbing Hopps.

Leatherbelly sat on Oyster's feet and started to
shake. The snake in the tree had spread its hinged
wings wide. It was gliding toward them, its dart-spitting
mouth wide open. Oyster tucked his head low again,
and whispered, from his heart, to Sister Mary Many

Pockets. *Will we find each other again? Will we?* He could hear a small *Yes* in his heart, and then the Yes grew louder and louder until it was a pounding Yes that shook the ground through his shoes.

Or perhaps it wasn't the Yes that was shaking the ground.

The Spike Balls stopped flying. The Blue Bats flitted off. The flying, Dart-Spitting Snake turned its wings and disappeared into the trees. Even the Jelly Roaches reversed their line toward Oyster's shoes. The pounding grew louder, and Oyster remembered. . . .

"Dragon," he said.

They all nodded, except Ringet, who started to read, " 'An ancient breed, the Dragon is most closely tied to—' "

"Stop it, Ringet! Stop! It's not going to help us now!"

From his spot in the bushes, Oyster could see the Dragon's large, curled nails; its giant, red-scaled haunches. Its red-crowned head reared up.

"Red?" Ippy said.

"Red?" Drusser added. "Never seen anything like it!"

"I have," said Oyster. It was much like the red dragon painted on the Dragon Palace at home. "My old world and this World—it's a translation," he explained.

Hopps was preparing his bow. "Doesn't matter. Either way, we're in trouble here."

"No," Drusser said. "An arrow will only make it angrier."

"It'll distract it enough for you all to run," Hopps said.

"But what about you?" Ringet asked.

"No," Ippy said. "It's too risky."

"We have to stick together," Oyster said.

Hopps didn't listen. He stood up, took aim, and shot. The arrow lodged itself in the Dragon's meaty shoulder, setting the mighty beast off balance for a moment. But there was no time to run. The Dragon quickly righted itself and bounded for Hopps. Hopps turned to run, but the Dragon clawed his back in one swipe.

"Hopps!" Ringet cried.

Hopps fell to the ground. The back of his Orwise Suspar and Sons Refinery uniform was clawed through, but he wasn't bleeding. He played dead while the Dragon leaned over the others. The Dragon cocked its crowned head and glared down at them with one glassy eye on the side of its horned face.

And then Ringet stood up. He put his hands on his bony hips. He drew in an enormous breath and he screamed. This scream was nothing like the one he'd let loose when the Goggle ate his hat. This scream was loud and long and piercing.

The Dragon stumbled backward, staggered until it lost its balance completely. It fell to its haunches and then collapsed in a heap. Its eyes closed. Its heavy breaths stopped.

"Ringet!" Oyster said, breathless. His own heart was still pounding in his chest.

Ippy said, "You killed a Dragon!"

Ringet was dazed. He dropped his hands off his hips and stood there, quite still and wide-eyed. His voice was just a chirp. "I did?"

Hopps stood up. "You did, Ringet."

Leatherbelly yipped triumphantly.

"Ippy's never killed a Dragon that quick," Drusser said.

Ippy tightened her eyes and glared at Drusser.

"What? It's true," Drusser said.

"It felt good," Ringet said. "To, you know, rise up like that!"

Hopps had his back to Ringet. He was dusting off his shirt.

"The Dragon clawed off some of the letters on the back of your uniform," Ippy said. "You're lucky to be alive. It was that close!"

"Really?" Hopps said.

Ringet picked up his paperback, stuffed it in his pocket. He looked at Hopps's back. "It felt good to rise up," he said again. And then his cheeks went red. His finger flew into the air. He turned around, pacing. He looked fevered. "I've got something," he said.

Hopps looked at him. "What is it, Ringet? You look strange. I don't know if I've ever seen you like this."

"I've got to go back to Boneland," Ringet said. "I know how to make the Perths rise up."

"It's not possible," Ippy said. "They don't have it in them."

Drusser shook his head. "Doggers, yes. Perths, no. They can't rise up."

"I will convince them," Ringet said.

"How?" Oyster asked.

"I can't explain it now. No time. They just need unity. That's all," Ringet said.

Hopps looked at Ringet with a steady eye. "Ringet," he said. "You've changed."

"I think I have!" Ringet said.

"But Ringet," Hopps said, "what if we do meet up with Eshma Weegrit. You won't be here to have your lock leg cured."

"I thought you didn't believe she was alive," Ippy said.

"Well, stranger things have happened," Hopps said, pointing to the Dragon.

"It doesn't matter about my leg," Ringet said. "There are more important things now."

Hopps turned to Drusser. "Can you lead Ringet back through the tunnels to Boneland? He needs a guide."

"I can," Drusser said. "Of course."

"We've got to go right now," Ringet said. "Will you be okay?" he asked Hopps.

Hopps grabbed his arm. "Sure," he said. "I'll be fine if this Eshma Weegrit shows up."

"She will," Ippy said.

"She will," Ringet agreed.

Hopps nodded.

Ringet limped down the trail with Drusser at his side. They both stopped and looked back.

Drusser gave a quick salute.

Ringet put his finger to the side of his nose.

Oyster, Ippy, and Hopps all saluted back and tapped their noses. Leatherbelly tossed back his head and gave a quick bark.

"Be careful," Hopps called out.

Ringet and Drusser started back down the path and then both dipped out of sight.

CHAPTER 19
ESHMA WEEGRIT'S CURES

Oyster, Hopps, Ippy, and Leatherbelly didn't stand for long in the charred clearing in front of the pile of turtle shells surrounded by the fried trees with the dead Dragon laid out before them. From the other side of the dead Dragon, with a snapping of twigs and a shuffling of footsteps, an old woman with a tuft of white cloudy hair appeared. Her hair seemed to follow behind her in a breathy fluff. When she stopped, it caught up and sat airily atop her head.

She patted the red-scaly back haunch of the Dragon and said, "Nice color work. Your doing, no doubt, Oyster?"

Oyster shrugged. "I guess so. Who are—"

"My, my, he was a big eater. Wasn't he, Ippy?"

"Eshma Weegrit!" Ippy announced proudly.

"In the flesh!" Eshma said. "Or, well now, I'm more

spirit than flesh these days, it seems. I'm on my way out.
But I'm still here."

"This is Hopps," Ippy said. "And Oyster and
Leatherbelly."

Hopps was flustered. He didn't like to be wrong.

"I—I, well, so nice to m-m . . . I've heard things. Nice things. It's . . ." He stalled out and shrugged.

"I know, I know. Understood. Hello, Hopps, dear man full of doubt, and the boy, of course. We've been waiting! And the small, paunchy beast. Nice to see you all."

Oyster was surprised that Eshma had been waiting for him! He thought it was the other way around. He was surprised to hear Leatherbelly described as paunchy. Oyster looked at the dachshund and noticed that Leatherbelly's stomach was indeed only a paunch. With all of the running around to survive, his belly had shrunk and no longer dragged on the ground.

"Um, excuse me. There's something quite urgent," Oyster said. "Sister Mary Many Pockets, she came for me, and she's in danger, and—"

"Oh, Oyster, do you doubt the woman of many pockets?" Eshma asked. "The Blood-Beaked Vultures didn't eat her. No, no. They were no match for her."

"Is she alive? Is she okay?" Oyster asked.

"Oh, yes. You see, she flapped and squawked. Her black cloth rose around her. She puffed her cheeks until her own face was a darker red than their own beaks. And they were afraid. They were very afraid. The vultures thought that she was an even larger, more terrifying bird. They flew away. She's actually a step ahead of you all. She's nearing Dark Mouth's

Torch. But perhaps if we hurry, you all will be able to catch up."

"How do you know all of this?" Oyster asked.

"I have ways of seeing. Don't you know that she's a woman of great strength?"

"I guess I do," Oyster said. He'd never thought of her like that before. She was always a woman of great fears—that's why he was never allowed beyond the nunnery gate. But he wasn't as afraid as he'd been either. Maybe they were both changing.

Eshma said, "Ippy, come over here and lay your hands on this Dragon's sunken chest. We've got to bring him back."

"To life?" Hopps blurted.

"I can't have the Dragon Perths angry. They don't like to lose a Dragon. But he'll be a sweetie when he revives. I'll make sure his spirits are high. Ippy, can you do this for me?"

"Are you sure? Me?" Ippy asked.

"Yes, yes," Eshma said. "Do you recall the mantra?"

Ippy nodded, but for the first time, she seemed scared to Oyster, and he realized that Eshma and Ippy knew each other well. Was Ippy learning to be a guru? "You can do it, Ippy," Oyster said. He was sure that Ippy could do most anything.

She looked at Oyster. "You think so?"

He nodded.

"I'd do it myself," Eshma said, "but I need to attend to Mr. Hopps, the man who has doubted me."

Hopps tried to correct her. "I've really come around. I mean, I believe in you plenty. I mean . . ."

While Ippy stared intently at the Dragon, Eshma ignored Hopps's blathering and pulled a blue vial from her pocket. "Here we are. This will sting just a bit," she said to Hopps. She uncorked the vile. Oyster sidled over for a closer look. Eshma poured some of the liquid on Hopps's gash.

Hopps bellowed and fell to his knees.

Eshma sighed and shrugged. "Oh, well. Sometimes healing is more painful than wounding," she explained.

Oyster watched the broken skin fold together and seal over with a new pinkish shine. The rip in Hopps's uniform knitted itself up; and in moments it was as if the Goggle had never bitten Hopps, as if the Dragon hadn't swiped at him. Hopps was panting, but the pain was gone. He touched his arm.

"Miraculous!" he said.

"Yes, yes, quite," Eshma said, unimpressed. "How's it coming, Ippy? Are you concentrating, dear?"

"I'm trying!" Ippy said.

"Draw up your strength, Ippy," Eshma said. "You can do this."

Ippy had her arms stretched, her head bowed. She was kneeling before the Dragon's ribs. She murmured under her breath. And then her hair began to rise. The Dragon's first breath, a deep inhale, was pulling her hair toward its wide nostrils. Ippy looked up at the Dragon's face, astonished.

"Good, good!" Eshma encouraged. "Excellent, dear!"

Hopps and Oyster shrank away from the Dragon. Leatherbelly's tail disappeared between his legs. The one eye of the Dragon that Oyster could see flipped open. It raised its heavy head. Ippy jumped up and ran to Oyster at the edge of the clearing.

But Eshma walked up to the Dragon and smiled. She walked over to a log, and, with little effort, she heaved the log up. She tapped the log on the ground. "Here, fella! Here, boy!"

The Dragon's tail pounded the ground.

And then Eshma hoisted up the log and threw it across the clearing.

The Dragon bounced up and bounded after it.

Eshma brushed her hands on her skirt. "I'd have one as a pet, but I hear they're impossible to house-train."

Hopps stepped forward. He gaped at the Dragon gnawing on the log and at Ippy, who was staring at her hands, amazed at what they'd done. He was holding his own arm, now healed. He spoke in a rattled voice—a little dry, shaken voice. "It was you, really, who saved us from the Dragon in the first place, wasn't it?"

Eshma let out a little laugh, then just smiled and lowered her chin. "Did you think it was the fella who screamed at the top of his lungs?"

Hopps shook his head. "No, no, 'course not." But Oyster knew that Hopps had thought the same thing that he had: Ringet had killed the Dragon with a scream.

"Don't tell the fella, now," Eshma said. "He needed the boost, didn't he?"

"He did," Hopps said. "He sure did."

"He's a changed man for it!" Eshma added.

Oyster was awed by Eshma Weegrit. "How did you do it?" he asked.

"Do what?" Eshma asked.

"Well, all of it!" Oyster asked.

"It's complicated," Ippy said. "It takes years of study."

"And in some ways, it isn't complicated at all," Eshma said. "What it comes down to is simple imagination."

"I'm not very good at that," Oyster said.

"Maybe you weren't good at that once upon a time, but I'm not worried about your imagination, Oyster. Not one bit."

Me neither, Ippy's heart said to Oyster.

This made Oyster feel a bit better. He knew there

were things that had to have come from him. He thought of the nunlike snores of the Breathing River; and Mrs. Fishback, alive in a strange way in the field of flowers; and Dr. Fromler's smile on Vince Vance's face; and the red Dragon. But this was his parents' World, wasn't it? "Did my parents create you?" he asked Eshma.

Eshma winked. "They marked a small X in a spot, here in the forest, and they put a single word: *guru*. And then I made myself!"

Oyster thought of his spindly little map in Ringet's oversized soup can, and then his mind just started running. He thought of the inside of the house: his parents in the kitchen making dinner together, and how he'd be able to hear his parents laughing in the background while he'd be in his bedroom, complete with a train set on the floor and a set of bunk beds, playing with his friend from the Dragon Palace, and how they would call him down for dinner when the time came . . . and what would that be like?

Eshma now trudged into the woods a bit. "Let's find the X. Come along!"

They followed behind her quickly. She was looking at the ground like she'd lost something.

"Do you see it, Ippy?" Eshma asked.

"Not yet," Ippy said.

"What are we looking for?" Oyster asked.

But Eshma didn't need to answer. "Aha!" she cried out. She picked up what looked like a golden stone from the ground, but it wasn't a golden stone at all. It was Eshma Weegrit's doorknob; and when she lifted it, a door swung wide, a door built into the ground, a door covered with moss and rocks and sticks.

CHAPTER 20

ESHMA WEEGRIT'S KEYS

When the door on the ground opened, a glowing light poured forth. Eshma paid no attention to it. She simply walked down a set of narrow steps. "Welcome," she said. "I have some things you'll need."

Hopps and Ippy went down first. Oyster and Leatherbelly followed. It was so bright inside that Oyster had to squint. The kitchen was small and dotted with brilliant lights. Oyster couldn't tell what these lights were. Some were roving overhead. Others were parked on counters and shelves. Others still were scurrying around on the floorboards. There were hundreds of them, maybe thousands.

Oyster was about to ask what they were, but Hopps blurted the answer. "Wingers!" he cried out. Oyster looked over at his well-lit face. His eyes were filled with tears. A few spilled onto his cheeks. "How many?" he said. "How many have you saved?"

"Didn't you know?" Ippy said.

"I thought they were all dead!" Hopps cried.

"Oh, no," Eshma said, walking through the bright kitchen, turning down a long, narrow hall. "I've saved a small nation. They're ready to rebuild."

Leatherbelly was confused by the Wingers, the small Perths with glowing chests. They flitted around his head and he pawed at them.

"Come on, Leatherbelly," Oyster said.

They were all careening as quickly as possible, following Eshma through a maze of halls. The Wingers got more plentiful, and the house grew brighter.

A mosquito-singing voice spoke from the floor. "Hopps? Is it you?" the voice whined, high-pitched. A Winger zipped up to Hopps's face and stopped abruptly.

"Ezbit?" Hopps said. "Ezbit? You're alive!" Hopps held out his hand, and Ezbit landed on it. Oyster's eyes were fixed on the Winger. His wings calmed and his chest went dim.

"Yes. I barely survived. My group took off for the valley. Eshma picked us up there and brought us to safety."

"Well, it's good to see you, my friend. Very good."

"Keep up!" Ippy said.

Hopps started walking again. Oyster and Leatherbelly did, too. Ezbit flitted up from his hand. "Are you going to defeat Dark Mouth with the boy?" he asked.

"Is that what's being said?"

Ezbit nodded. "That's the boy, isn't it?"

"Yes," Hopps said.

"Good luck," Ezbit said.

"I'm glad you're alive," Hopps said.

"I'm ready to go home," Ezbit said. "We all are." There was a chirruping chorus of Wingers. "We're cheering you all on!" Ezbit said. He put his finger to his nose and looked at Oyster, who returned the gesture. "The boy!" Ezbit said. "At long last!"

Oyster wasn't sure what to make of this. He didn't feel like he'd done anything to help so far. He wanted to confess that he'd lost the Slippery Map. He wanted to be a hero, of course, but he wasn't comfortable with so many people depending on him.

"The boy!" the Winger cheered, his tiny wings beating fiercely in the air. "The boy!"

"Here we are," Eshma said, turning into the last room at the end of the hall. "The key room!"

The key room was properly named. It was filled with keys of all shapes and sizes. When Eshma opened the door, it created a little breeze that stirred the hanging keys, rows of them, and they all chimed noisily. The room smelled dank and metallic.

"You have keys?" Hopps asked. "To what?" He was inspecting keys, one after the other, turning them and looking at their numbers.

"She has keys to everything!" Ippy said. "I told you she would help us."

"Keys to the jail cells. The specific key to Oyster's parents' joint cell. The key to Dark Mouth's inner compound that leads to the tower," Eshma said breezily. "Keys, keys, keys."

Hopps stopped. "Wait just a minute. You could have gotten into Dark Mouth's inner compound? How many times over could you have killed him?"

"I'm a guru." Eshma looked at Hopps. Her chin tucked to her chest, she eyed him sternly. "I've taken vows to give aid to the sickly. Dark Mouth, poor in health, is my patient. I'm not a murderer."

Oyster glanced around the room. Keys hung from poles striping the ceiling, lit by darting Wingers. Boxes filled with keys sat on the floor. The walls all had built-in drawers and cabinets. Those that were open showed only more keys. They were all numbered and in some kind of order, Oyster could tell. Somewhere among all of the keys was the key that could free his parents. "Do you know my parents?" Oyster asked. "Have you seen them? Are they okay?"

"Your mother has headaches sometimes. Your father has to watch his blood pressure. Other than that they're fit," Eshma said.

"And, and"—he turned back to Eshma—"couldn't you have freed them? If you have the key . . ."

Ippy looked at Oyster. "Maybe they don't want to be freed. Not like that. Not with a trick of a key. My parents died in the Foul Revolution. If your parents snuck out of jail and the Perths didn't rise up for themselves with their own muscle, then it would be like my parents died for nothing."

Oyster felt a surge of panic. Didn't his parents want, more than anything, to be with him? He was confused. Hopps was too.

"What are you talking about?" Hopps shouted. "You don't know what you're saying. If they could get free, they would. They'd help us! They'd make us rise up!"

Eshma said, "The uprising must come from the Perths themselves. They understand that. If it doesn't come from within, if they don't rise up and convince themselves of their own strength, then they'll just fall again. If not beaten down by Dark Mouth, then by someone else."

Oyster let his eyes wander around the room: keys, Wingers, shuffling lights, glinting metal teeth. He felt dizzy. "But how could they not want to be free? Don't they want to raise me?"

"They are raising you, Oyster. They're raising you to be a force, someone who can live by his wits and survive," Eshma said. "Someone who will one day be able to lead. Don't you see that?"

Oyster shook his head. "No," he said. "That's not right. It's not fair." He thought of Sister Mary Many Pockets, and how she cared for him. He thought of her face beaming at him, even when he was in a bit of trouble, even when he'd come flying out of the broom closet and his moth collection, led by his pet bird, flew through the kitchen, even when all of the nuns were disgusted by him and wanted their peace, even when the Vicious Goggles were taking her away to be fed to Blood-Beaked Vultures. "No," Oyster said again.

"Well," Hopps said, "I'll take the keys: to Dark Mouth's inner compound, all of the jail cells. Ringet said he could get the Perths to rise up. He might be telling the truth. It's now or never—for me, anyway. The Goggles by now already know I'm gone. They'll be after me." He patted Oyster on the back. "It's now or never for you, too, Oyster. Don't you see it?"

Oyster nodded.

Eshma walked to a cabinet. She opened it with a tiny key from her pocket, then pulled open the bottom drawer. There was a metal box inside, padlocked. She twisted the lock through a combination—a long, complicated combination—then popped it open. Inside was a ring of keys, at least a hundred. She took a cloth sack sitting on top of the cabinet and filled it with a ring of narrow keys on a brass stick. "Start here," she said. "At cell one, first key after the stick. Oyster's parents are in cell forty-two."

"Forty-two," Oyster repeated.

She put the ring in the sack. "And this is the key to Dark Mouth's inner compound." From inside the metal box she pulled an enormous, ornate key that was long and gold and jagged. When she dropped it into the sack, it clanked against the smaller set. She handed the sack to Oyster.

"You're not coming?" Oyster asked Eshma.

"Ippy and I have come as far as we should," she said. "You are on your own now."

"Why?" Oyster said. "Ippy?"

"I'm going back to prepare the Doggers," Ippy said.

"I'll be here preparing the Wingers," Eshma said. "Everyone will be necessary in the end."

Oyster felt sick and weak. He swung the bag over his shoulder.

"The prisons are within the mountains," Eshma said. "You'll find air holes, part of a system of vents, while you climb. Dark Mouth's inner compound can be reached by a wide door at the base of the tower. You'll be fine."

Oyster wasn't so sure. The sack was already weighing him down.

Hopps sighed. "Eshma," he said, "I have a friend with a locked leg. The one who thought he'd killed the Dragon by screaming."

"And I know someone who has to wear leg braces, but he's far away," Oyster added. "Could you cure them?"

She nodded. "Perhaps. I'll try."

Oyster looked at Ippy. "Will we see each other again?" he asked.

"We will," she said. "And be careful, Oyster."

"You too," he said.

"It's a place of death and darkness," Eshma added. "Just follow the Torch."

CHAPTER 20½
A BRIEF INTERRUPTION . . .

Now, if you look closely at the Slippery Map—as Vince
Vance was at the very moment that Hopps, Oyster, and
Leatherbelly were heading out of Eshma Weegrit's
underground home—you will notice that wherever
someone has made a cut to create a portal through the
Slippery Map, there is a dimple left behind. A small
scar, one might say. And so, looking at the Map pinned
to a corkboard, Vince Vance was eyeing each of these
little dimple-scars quite closely. He had a handful of
pushpins, and one by one, he stuck them into the dim-
ples, hoping that they would lead him to the other side.

"Hollywood," he said. "Where is Hollywood?
Hollywood? Is this it? Is this?"

A certain Hula Hoop became dark and windy again—
as did a tire swing, a tunnel slide at a public pool (still
closed to the public), a soccer goal, and the innards of

a sofa. A gust escaped from Alvin Peterly's refrigerator box—which had become a neighborhood attraction that Alvin charged people one dollar each to peek into. But no one noticed. It was just a small pinprick of a portal—and, frankly, folks had lost interest in Alvin Peterly's refrigerator box and so it had been abandoned in his dusty garage.

One would think that Mrs. Fishback and Dr. Fromler would have noticed the pinprick of wind from the spitting sink—as they'd professed to be so dedicated to the return of Leatherbelly and devoted to teeth everywhere. They were actually in the office, eating candies together in exam room number one. But they were goo-y with each other—as is the case with people who've fallen in love—and so they didn't even notice the pinprick of windy gusts puffing up from the spitting sink.

In the nunnery, however, the nuns were carefully keeping an eye on the organ. They were praying day and night as hard as they could for some sort of sign. Sister Hilda Prone to Asthma was in charge of checking the broom closet. She'd set up a small kneeler there so she could keep up her prayers. She was the one to notice the first bits of a breeze. She was hot. It was summer. And at first, the breeze made her feel contented, and then she realized that maybe it was the beginning of an Awful MTD, so she ran to the chapel. The other nuns were gathered around the organ, because Sister Elouise of the Occasional Cigarette had detected the motion as well. They wanted to follow Sister Mary Many Pockets. They wanted to help find Oyster, but they weren't sure how to proceed.

And there was another problem, which Mother Superior pointed out in a note that she passed around: They weren't all together. Sister Margaret of the Long Sighs and Withering Glare was across the street at the Dragon Palace. They couldn't leave her behind even if they did know how to get to Oyster, which they didn't.

As you know, the nuns never went outside the nunnery gates except for special circumstances, such as the doctor or an emergency, but they'd gotten accustomed to ordering takeout from the Dragon Palace across the street. This was an emergency, Mother Superior had noted. There was no time for anything but prayer! And so every day, they wrote down their orders, left them at the register, and came to pick them up midday for lunch and in the early evening for dinner.

Sister Margaret of the Long Sighs and Withering Glare had already walked into the Dragon Palace, past the boy with the leg braces and the blue umbrella. She was squinting at the man behind the counter, who handed her a large, oil-stained bag of their take-out boxes when, all of a sudden, the boy with the blue umbrella started to shout.

"Help!" he cried out. "Help me!"

Sister Margaret of the Long Sighs and Withering Glare turned and ran for the boy. She was very sensitive now to the cries of children—she missed Oyster terribly. The boy's umbrella was gusting violently, whipping around his head, lifting him off of his little chair. Sister Margaret of the Long Sighs and Withering Glare was the first there. Still holding tight to her takeout order with one arm, she grabbed the boy around the middle and fought to keep him tethered to the ground. The boy's father and mother appeared behind her, shouting commands in Chinese. One can assume that they were saying something like, "Let go of the umbrella! Be careful!" and "Who is this woman in the long black dress and veil who always sighs and stares at us coldly every time she comes for her large pickup orders? And why is she trying to help?"

And you might have some questions too, such as, why all of a sudden is it not just a pinprick through the Map, but a big, windy portal?

Well, the answer is this: Vince Vance had grown more and more agitated, poking the pins into the dimple-scars. He'd gotten angrier and angrier. "Hollywood?" he kept saying, a loud mantra, "Hollywood?" And soon the Map had pins all over it, not just in the dimple-scars. And then he put the final pin into place: the Dragon Palace. He pushed it in hard and then twisted it angrily, making a mighty hole.

"Hollywood!" he screamed through the hole.

And that is what Sister Margaret of the Long Sighs and Withering Glare heard, and so did the boy and his parents.

"Hollywood?" the parents said to each other.

Sister Margaret of the Long Sighs and Withering Glare had yanked the boy to his parents and wrestled the umbrella from his fist. She let it drag her across the street, back to the nunnery gate. She opened the gate and pulled the gusty umbrella through the front door, the take-out order still held tight—she wasn't one to waste food. She made an awful clatter, battling the wild, bucking umbrella.

The nuns all came running. They understood immediately—not how or why Sister Margaret of the Long Sighs and Withering Glare had a portal in this blue umbrella—but what exactly they should do next.

Clutching their takeout and plasticware, the nuns stepped into the blue umbrella one at a time, and disappeared into the Gulf of Wind and Darkness. Mother Superior was the final nun. She dipped the toe of her rubber-soled shoe into the umbrella. There's one thing you should know about Mother Superior: She was raised in Kansas and, as a child, developed a fear of tornados. When she stepped into the umbrella and the wind swirled up her skirt, she held on to the blue umbrella and it snapped through its own portal. So as all of the nuns were sailing through the Gulf, Mother Superior was still clutching the blue umbrella. And the nunnery was empty and still, except for a little swirl of dust and then nothing.

And Vince Vance, you ask? What about him? He had a good cry, and then he took all of the pins out of the Map. He rolled it up—and, knowing that he hadn't found Hollywood and that he might never escape to find his fame—he did as he'd been ordered.

He made his way to Dark Mouth's tower so that he could deliver the Map.

Chapter 21
An Unlikely Trail

It was dark by the time Oyster, Hopps, and Leatherbelly got to the steepest part of the Pinch-Eye Mountains. Dark Mouth's Torch was the only light. It glowed in the night sky, making the shadows dart and waver so that it was hard to know where to get a handhold. Leatherbelly hadn't had the paws for it. He was in the sack with the keys, which Hopps had tied to his back. Every once in a while Leatherbelly let out a pitiful whine.

"Almost there," Hopps would tell him. This comforted Oyster the first few times he'd said it, but now he wasn't sure if they'd ever reach Dark Mouth's compound. The good news was that the harsh terrain didn't allow for the beasts they'd found below. The only creatures that could handle the steep and rocky incline were Many-Eyed Mountain Goats. They were eerie to look at, covered in their excess of eyes, but they were fairly tame creatures that looked on from a distance.

When Oyster gazed across the valley to the rise beyond, he could see ORWISE SUSPAR AND SONS REFINERY lit up in bright letters, looming above the puffing stacks. He wondered if Drusser and Ringet had made it back to Boneland, if they were safe on the other side, getting the uprising going.

In addition to the bag of keys, Eshma had given them some meat-paste sandwiches and a water jug, which they'd finished. Oyster was hungry again, though, and his legs were burning and trembling from the climb.

When Hopps saw the first air hole, he pointed it out. "Getting close," he said.

The air hole was protected by a slatted vent cover like the heating ducts in the nunnery. Oyster imagined the channels dug out underground and how each led to a cell—and how one led to cell number forty-two, where his parents had lived for many years. It was strange to be so close to them. He realized he was scared to see them. How would they react? He wanted so much from them—all the love he'd missed his whole life. His chest felt heavy with all of his wanting.

He said, "Let's stop a minute, Hopps."

Hopps was tired too. He pulled the sack off his back and sat on a rocky ledge. Leatherbelly nosed his way from the opening and looked around, wide-eyed.

"We'll regain some energy," Hopps said.

"My parents are down there somewhere."

"I know," Hopps said.

"I'm scared," Oyster said. "What if I can't save them? What if they don't like me?"

Hopps turned to Oyster sharply. "Oyster," he said, "don't you know they love you?"

Oyster shrugged. "Then why did they hand me over to you, Hopps? Why didn't they bring me back through the Slippery Map so we could be together? They could have, couldn't they? Why didn't they do that?" Oyster's voice was tight in his throat.

Hopps shook his head. "They saved you, Oyster. It was hard then. The Foul Revolution. They loved you then, Oyster. They love you now."

Oyster felt heartsick, guilty for ever having doubted his parents, their love. They'd saved him. They'd made the right choice. "I want to see them," he said. "With my own eyes." He sat near a vent covering and peered into it.

"There are prisoners under us," Hopps said. "Imagine, someone is down there, on the other side of this air hole. But not for long." He was slouching with fatigue. His face was wet with sweat. It glistened in the torchlight from overhead.

"I wonder who it is," Oyster said.

And then there was a hoarse whisper. It shot up

through the vent and was pushed into the night air. "Prisoner Five Seven Two Four. Olgand Preferous."

Oyster and Hopps were startled. They leaned in closer.

"Hello?" Oyster said.

"Few words. You're being looked for—you are a boy, yes? A boy with something called 'a dog'?"

"I'm Oyster, and Leatherbelly is with me. How did you know?"

"Fewer words. Hush. Notes slipped through vents. *Boy and dog, missing. Have you seen them?* We ate the notes. No evidence."

"Written on little slips of paper?" Oyster asked. "Little notes in slanted handwriting?"

"Yes."

Oyster turned to Hopps. "It's Sister Mary Many Pockets. She's looking for me."

Leatherbelly let out a hopeful bark.

"Are you saving us?" the voice said.

"We are. We are," Oyster said.

"He's not just any boy, missing. He's *the* boy!" Hopps explained.

"Are my parents there?" Oyster asked.

"Fewer words. Hush. Yes. Parents. We've been wait-ing. Keys?"

Oyster took this to mean that his parents were there,

somewhere, underground. "Yes, keys," Oyster said, trying to use as few words as possible.

"Pass through vent."

This made Oyster nervous. He'd been tricked before, giving the Slippery Map to Vince Vance. "No, Hopps," Oyster said. "What if he isn't Prisoner Five Seven Two Four? Olgand Preferous."

"Hopps?" the voice said, suddenly sounding chummy. "Is that you? Don't you remember me? I'm O. The O. From the old days."

"O? Old O, the Preferous Professor! Could it be you? I heard you disappeared. Is Oli and Marge's boy with you?"

There was a shuffling noise, a clanging, and then another voice. "I'm here, Mr. Hopps, sir. Are my parents okay?"

Hopps started to cry. He could barely get the words out. "They miss you," he said in a shaky voice. He wiped his teary eyes.

"Are you going to save us?" Oli and Marge's son asked.

"Fewer!" Ogland said.

"Yes," Hopps said. He dug the keys out from under Leatherbelly. The duct was slatted, but there was a screw in each of the four corners. They were a bit rusty, but loose enough to wheedle off. It was a square duct. Oyster held the ring of keys over it.

"Go ahead," Hopps said. "Let them go."

Oyster released his grip, and the ring of keys started its noisy, clattering descent, but nearly as soon as it started skidding and bumping through the twisting ductwork, it stopped.

"Keys?" Hopps asked.

"No," Ogland said.

Hopps looked at Oyster. "I think they got hung up on something."

"They're stuck?" Oyster's voice was dry, his throat tight.

"Problem?" the voice asked.

"No," Hopps said, then he turned to Oyster. "Maybe we can knock it loose." He picked up a rock and put it down the winding chute. It banged and banged, down and down and down.

"Rock," the voice said. "Not keys. Problem?" the voice said.

Oyster looked down the dark hole.

"It's hit a snag. Maybe it's hung up on a root that's pushed its way into the duct. It'll take more precise work to get it unhooked." Hopps looked at Leatherbelly. "No problem," he said.

"But there is a problem," Oyster whispered, "a big one."

"No, there isn't," Hopps said, pointing at Leatherbelly and then to the square hole. "The beast can do it. He has teeth. He can unhook the keys."

Leatherbelly, still inside the sack, tensed up. Oyster could feel him go rigid. "He can't. He won't fit," Oyster said.

Leatherbelly complained about this jab at his weight by giving a little growl.

"He'll fit," Hopps said, reaching over and pulling Leatherbelly out of the sack.

Leatherbelly's belly had firmed up. He'd been working hard. He was no longer the flabby dog in the nunnery kitchen.

But still Oyster didn't want him to go. He'd come to rely on Leatherbelly. They'd been through a lot. "How would we find him again?"

"He'll be a hero among the prisoners. When they're free, they will bring him with them, surely."

"He's not that kind of beast," Oyster said, but he wasn't so sure of that. Leatherbelly had fought Water Snakes and outrun Spider Wolves and Dragons. "Or, well, he didn't used to be."

Oyster looked down at Leatherbelly. Leatherbelly looked up at Oyster. He stuck out his narrow chin. He gave a nod.

"Okay, then," Oyster said, hefting the dog from his shirt.

Leatherbelly walked to the hole, solemn as a soldier. He peered down the chute, looked back to Oyster and

Hopps once, just once, and then stepped into the chute and began to skid along himself. They listened to Leatherbelly careen down, but not very far. He seemed to stop at around the same place as the keys.

There was silence, then a small grunt, and then the glorious sound of a dog skidding along ductwork accompanied by the occasional clatter of metal on metal. *Ah, Leatherbelly, the hero,* Oyster thought, imagining Leatherbelly with the key ring in his teeth. *Who would have ever guessed it?*

There was a solid *thud,* and then the voice again. "Got 'em!"

The only thing left in the sack was the key that unlocked Dark Mouth's inner compound.

"Go. Danger. They know you come. Thank you," the voice said.

Oyster whispered to Hopps, "They know you come? Do you think Dark Mouth is waiting for us too? He must be."

Hopps sighed. "He knows."

Oyster felt sick. He wiped some sweat from his forehead. "We'll never win," he said.

Hopps put his hands on his hips, secured the sack on his back again, and looked at his boots. Then he bent over to examine something on the ground. "What's this?" he said. Hopps pointed out a small weed that had

bullied its way up from a crevice in the packed dirt.

"A weed?" Oyster said.

"Touch it," Hopps said.

Oyster did. The weed didn't bend to his touch. It was stiff, brittle, as if held in a little calcified casement. "It feels like tiny bones," Oyster said.

"It has turned to bone," Hopps explained. "This is a place of death and darkness. Remember? Ringet told you about the giant twenty-foot High-Tipping Bluebells, the Rosy-Upsies, the old garden that was destroyed for Dark Mouth's Torch. Do you recall it?"

"The petals used to float into the valley like blankets," Oyster said.

"Yes, yes, that's it. Well, Ringet told you that Dark Mouth had killed everything, turned it all to bone. Here it is. Our first real sign. We're close now."

They both stared up at the Torch. "It's too big," Oyster said. "It's too tall. How will we ever put it out?"

Hopps shook his head. "I don't know, Oyster. But we have to. That is how the Perths will know that his reign has ended." He lowered his voice to a whisper. "I'm afraid of Dark Mouth, massive, pale, his mouth a dark hole. Just a little afraid."

Oyster touched the weed again. "Will he turn us to bone, Hopps? Is that what he does?"

Hopps didn't want to answer. His face twisted. He was holding his breath.

"Is that what he does?"

Hopps nodded. "That, yes, or you go underground in the prison for the rest of your life."

Oyster wanted to go back into the valley. He didn't want to go on. His parents didn't really need him, did they? All of the prisoners could free themselves now. Even if he didn't find the Slippery Map and never made it home again, at least he wouldn't be made of pure bone.

The Torch flickered and light fell for a second on something else sitting near the weed. Oyster squinted at it in the dim light. He picked up a small, brown, dimpled husk, busted open. It sat in his palm. He looked up at the remaining cliff. There was a littered trail.

"It's a peanut shell!" Oyster explained. "A peanut shell." Oyster had no choice. He had to go on. Sister Mary Many Pockets was on her way to Dark Mouth. Oyster had gotten her into this. He'd have to get her out. He hopped up and started following the trail.

"What is it?" Hopps said, scrambling after him. "Oyster?"

CHAPTER 22

DARK MOUTH'S INNER COMPOUND

A few peanut shells sat in a small heap at the wide door on the side of Dark Mouth's tower. Oyster and Hopps had the key to this door. It was in the sack on Hopps's back. Sister Mary Many Pockets didn't have a key and so the trail of peanut shells continued on behind a row of stiff bone-bushes.

"We shouldn't use the key," Oyster said. "They're waiting for us. Ogland said so."

Hopps agreed. By now, Oyster had explained that the peanut shells belonged to Sister Mary Many Pockets. Hopps already had great respect for her since Eshma had told them that she'd scared off the Blood-Beaked Vultures and survived. Oyster and Hopps followed the trail of peanut shells behind the bone-bushes to a broken window. It was unlike Sister Mary Many Pockets to break a window. All of the nuns were very upset when someone broke one of their windows, which happened from time to time. But Oyster reminded himself that these were desperate times.

Oyster and Hopps helped each other through the window and inside a dimly lit circular stairwell. The air was cold and damp.

They tiptoed up the dark turning stairs until they came to what first appeared to be a row of lamps lining the hallway. But then there were small voices, saying, "Is it time?" "Is that the boy?" "Will you save us?"

Oyster leaned in close to one of the lamps and saw that it was actually a small cage mounted on the wall with Wingers inside.

"Are you okay?" Oyster asked, examining the cage's lock.

"We've heard that it's time," a female Winger said. "True?"

Another Winger in a cage a few steps up chimed in, "Will you save us?"

"Of course," Hopps said. He pulled a sharp tool out of his sack. "Step back," he said. The Wingers in the cage pressed their backs against the far bars. Hopps wedged the tool between the bars and pried them open, leaving enough space for the Wingers to fly out.

"Thank you!" they cried.

Hopps looked up the long rows of ascending cages. "We don't have enough time to save you all right now," he said. "But I promise, we will."

"If we live," Oyster added.

Hopps quickly pried open another cage's bars, setting Wingers loose.

"Where's your army?" the female Winger asked.

"It's just us, I think," Oyster said. "And a nun. Did you see one go by?"

The Winger from the next cage over stuck her face between the bars. "Are nuns short and wide and wearing black dresses and long hats that fall on their backs?"

"Yes," Oyster said. "Was one here?"

The Winger looked sad. "Yes, they took her to the Torch."

"The Torch?" Hopps asked. "She's with Dark Mouth?"

"Straight up there," another Winger said. "She put up some fight."

Oyster looked up the winding stairs. "They've got her already."

"And now," Hopps said, working a hole in another set of bars, "they know they've got you. They know you'll come for her."

"Well," Oyster said, "they're right. Nothing else to do."

"Right," he said.

"We can help," said one of the Wingers set loose. "We can be messengers. We can tell the others that you need help."

"Do you know Eshma and Ippy?"

They all nodded.

"Tell them to hurry," Oyster said. "Thank you."

The Wingers flew off with great haste while Oyster and Hopps continued to climb the tower stairs.

Oyster wondered if Sister Mary Many Pockets had already been served to Vicious Goggles. He wondered if Vince Vance would be here with Dark Mouth, if he would still have the Slippery Map. He wanted to know, once and for all, what Dark Mouth looked like. He wanted to tell him just what he thought of him. But when he came to the landing where the stairs stopped at a pair of closed iron doors and saw the ground dotted with peanuts—whole and shelled—he imagined that Sister Mary Many Pockets had fought hard, and he was scared.

This door didn't have a lock, just two enormous cast iron knockers.

"Should we knock?" Oyster asked.

Hopps shook his head. " 'Course not! Surprise attack!"

"There's no surprise for them now." Oyster picked up

the knocker and let it drop. The doors instantly opened onto a short set of stairs. Overhead, they could see the night sky lit by the fiery Torch. They walked up the last set of stairs slowly, and found themselves standing at the top of the tower. All Oyster could see at first was white, a dusty white presence, at least ten times his size. There were Vicious Goggles, a ghastly row of teeth and restless tongues, guarding the presence—but what was it? Slowly he could make out the stone wall around the circular tower, the wood floor, and the vast view of the valley, and on the other side of the valley, the Orwise Suspar and Sons Refinery sign, glowing in the haze of sugar. Boneland looked like a small village caught in a snow globe.

In the center of the tower was the Torch, lit with a great fire on top. The chalky white mass seemed to have grown around the Torch—the way bread dough will puff and spill out around an object. Was this Dark Mouth? Oyster couldn't make out any features, only whiteness.

The Torch was surrounded by even taller flowers. They were the tallest, grandest flowers Oyster had ever seen—but they were pale and stiff an turned to bone.

Oyster and Hopps stood side by side, and then Vince Vance's voice boomed. "Welcome to the Dark Mouth Show! Starring the beloved Dark Mouth . . . with the minor roles going to a boy and his beast, plus an embarrassing trio, pathetic in size and stature, and an old woman who appears from nowhere, trying to save the day. Tonight's show, the grand finale, promises to be heart-wrenching! A real tearjerker." Vince Vance emerged from the shadows behind the large white form, holding a long sword like a staff. He held out his arm and a bunch of Vicious Goggles herded out Sister Mary Many Pockets so that she stood between the white mass on one side and Oyster and Hopps on the other.

Hopps stood stiff, his eyes darting nervously around the room. But Oyster had locked eyes with Sister Mary Many Pockets. They were speaking in the rushed urgent language of their hearts.

You came to save me and look what I've gotten you into! Oyster's heart said.

Have faith, Oyster. We aren't sunk yet. There's breath in our lungs and love in our hearts.

I don't want to lose you again, sister!

Oyster, her heart said, *love goes on forever, in all directions, and our love for each other here—it's just a sample. There is so much love for you! So much! The world has only begun to show you, only just begun. Your parents, Oyster . . .*

Oyster's heart seized. He hadn't wanted her to know about them. He thought that it would hurt her feelings that he'd come all this way, in part, to know them.

We can all love you.

The white mass lolled slowly, menacingly, revealing two dark holes—perhaps its eyes—nearly lost in the hefty rolls of what was now clearly a face. A hollow appeared below the eyes: a black, toothless mouth, a dark pit. Oyster was terrified of the mouth. It spoke. "I am a giant force. I am a hale source of evil. And I am hungry."

Hopps's ire rose up. He couldn't help it. "Don't you have enough sugar to eat! We make it for you day and night. We're dying across that valley, dying because we have to feed you."

"Tonight I will eat something other than sugar!" Dark Mouth said in a voice so deep and loud that Oyster could feel the vibrations in his ribs.

A metal arm swung out from the stone Torch. Two figures were tied to a hook at the end of the arm—a sharp, silver hook. A man and a woman.

They looked so ordinary. The man had pale eyebrows and a soft face. The woman had long brown hair and a furrowed brow. Maybe to someone else, they looked like two people from anywhere, two people plucked from their sofas in the middle of the afternoon watching an old movie—in their cardigan sweaters. (His mother's was missing a few buttons.) But they weren't just anyone from anywhere. They were Oyster's parents.

He had his mother's dark hair and his father's rounded face. They were both weary, but their eyes were quick— desperately so—and they fell on Oyster almost immediately. Then their eyes filled with tears, their faces broke open into an expression of joy and sorrow. They looked at Oyster with so much love that he could barely keep his eyes on them, but he did. He drank in the love. They were his parents.

"You can't do this!" Hopps yelled.

And then Oyster realized that his parents were dangling near the black hole on Dark Mouth's face. They bobbed on the metal hook.

Dark Mouth spoke again. "Bring out the Slippery Map."

Vince Vance had the Slippery Map in his arms, but it was bucking like something wild—much worse than it had when Sister Mary Many Pockets had been lodged inside of the Gulf of Wind and Darkness. It jumped and spun and pounded with such force that Vince Vance was kicked around by it. The rowdiness of the Map cheered Oyster a bit. Last time it had been Sister Mary Many Pockets come to save him . . . and this time?

"Roll it out!" Dark Mouth shouted.

Vince Vance dropped it on the floor in front of Oyster and flipped it open as far as it would go in either direction, but still it jumped and bounced wildly. With a poke of his sword, Vince Vance ordered Goggles to sit on either end to keep it taut.

"Let's see how it works," Vince Vance said. "Do you want him to make a passage? So you can slip through to the other side?"

"No," Dark Mouth said. "I want to destroy it!"

Destroy it? This surprised everyone. Didn't he want to go through it to rule on the other side? Didn't he want to take over? Wasn't his greed without limit?

"But, but," Vince Vance said, nearly in tears, "I thought we were going through!"

"I never said that!" Dark Mouth roared.

"You can't destroy the Map," Hopps said. "It's how we were created. It's our history!"

"It doesn't belong to you," Oyster said.

Sister Mary Many Pockets was wringing her hands. She was thinking the same things that Oyster was thinking. *Who was inside of the Gulf of Wind and Darkness? Wouldn't they be trapped? And if the Map was destroyed, how would they get home again?* The Map rattled and jerked thunderously.

"I want this Map destroyed, and you will be the one to do it, Oyster," Dark Mouth said. "YOU!"

Oyster looked up at Dark Mouth, but he felt his eyes burning and tearing up.

"Do it now!" Dark Mouth shouted.

His parents stared at him. They nodded in a way that said, *Do what you have to do.*

Sister Mary Many Pockets told him, with her heart, to listen to his own.

Hopps stood still. "It's your decision, Oyster."

"Give him your sword!" Dark Mouth shouted to Vince Vance.

Vince Vance handed it to him. Oyster couldn't let his parents and then Hopps, Sister Mary Many Pockets, and himself get eaten. But he couldn't destroy the Map either.

Oyster looked up, one last time, at those who were waiting. He thought of brave Leatherbelly, wherever his bravery had taken him. They loved him. They trusted him. And he didn't feel lonesome. He didn't feel like an outsider. He belonged to these people, this odd group. He had to do what he had to do, but he had a plan.

He raised the sword overhead, but then backed up and let it gently swing down to the surface of the Map, and then he gave the center a little jab.

The Map, however, was ready to burst. Like a crack in ice shattering across a lake, the hole expanded and split up the center. It opened wide, a monstrous, gaping hole.

A wind kicked up, and then a body popped out. Another flew after it, and another and another. They soared out of a giant hole in the map: Sister Elizabeth Thick Glasses, Sister Margaret of the Long Sighs and Withering Glare, Sister Clare of the Mighty Flyswatter, Sister Alice Self-Defense, Sister Helen Quick Fingers, Sister Bertha Nervous Lips, Sister Hilda Prone to Asthma, Sister Patricia Tough-Pork, Sister Augusta of the Elaborate Belches, Sister Elouise of the Occasional Cigarette, Sister Theresa Raised on a Farm, and even Mother Superior, still clutching the blue umbrella. They were tossed up and out, and landed in heaps across the flooring.

But each nun jumped quickly to her feet, spry and ready. They had their stiff hands ready to chop an attacker in two, their knees bent. They'd been preparing for an attacker for years, and Sister Alice Self-Defense looked steely eyed; she was confident in her troop.

Meanwhile, the Map had been ripped in two. Its halves snapped and rolled into themselves. Oyster felt sick. He looked to Hopps, but he just shook his head sadly. Oyster's parents, too, had let out a gasp. Oyster knew that the Map was ruined. It couldn't be fixed.

Dark Mouth laughed. "It is destroyed after all, and this is who has come to save you? Ha!"

Vince Vance knelt next to the Map. "Can it be mended?" he asked in a quavering voice.

"Leave the Map, Vince Vance. Look at it. It is limp

and powerless now. These people want to do battle. Let's enjoy! This is all they've got!"

"No," Hopps said. "This is not all!" He pointed down the valley to Boneland on the other side. The Orwise Suspar and Sons Refinery sign was missing some letters. It now read: R ISE U P   FINE. And even at this great distance, they could hear the chants of "Rah-rah! Hoot-hoot!" from the Perths of Boneland.

"Ringet!" Hopps said. "He did it! He convinced them to rise up, using the sign itself!" Oyster thought of the letters left behind on the back of Hopps's uniform after the Dragon took its angry swipe. So that's what Ringet was thinking about, how to get the Perths united, using the lights from the refinery.

Vince Vance said, "It will take hours for them to reach us."

"And by then, you'll all be eaten up!" Dark Mouth said.

"I'm not so sure," Oyster said. Because that wasn't all either. That's when the banging at the door below began: The prisoners were free. Oyster was overjoyed to hear Leatherbelly's shrill barks amid the noise of pounding fists. Some Vicious Goggles rushed down the small set of steps to try to hold them back.

And then from the valley, a great light was appearing. Wingers, an army of them, rode up toward the tower.

They carried Eshma Weegrit through the air and set her down next to Hopps. The rest of the Wingers buzzed in. The prisoners, more Wingers among them, at last bashed their way through the doors and then were overpowering the Goggles with fists and shoves. They stormed up the steps.

The Vicious Goggles surrounding Dark Mouth froze. Dark Mouth howled, "Do something!"

Vince Vance looked around nervously, then pulled a dagger from his boot and jabbed at the air in front of him. "Stay back!" he shouted. "Back!"

"And we're not done yet!" Hopps was shouting because a loud whine had started from underground. It was a noise that Oyster recognized. Growsels, with their hooked claws, were scaling the tower, with Doggers on their backs. They climbed over the tower walls, hundreds of them—Drusser and Ippy leading the way.

"We're here!" Drusser shouted, as the Doggers pulled arrows from their quivers and took aim at Dark Mouth and Vince Vance.

Ippy shook dirt from her hair. "This is the way it was meant to happen, Oyster."

Dark Mouth bellowed, "This is war! Commence!"

And so the Goggles started flinging their angry tongues while more poured into the tower. It was an angry fight. Drusser and Ippy had extra bows and quivers filled with arrows for Oyster and Hopps. Oyster wasn't a great shot at first, but he caught on quickly. Leatherbelly fought with his teeth, snapping at Goggle legs.

And the nuns were in the thick of it. Oyster saw them in a way he never had before. Sister Alice Self-Defense and the others flipped Goggles over their backs and kicked them in their soft kidneys. Sister Helen Quick Fingers grabbed tongues midair and, with her bare hands, knit them together. Sister Clare of the Mighty Flyswatter and Sister Elouise of the Occasional Cigarette were both roped by tongues, but Sister Clare smacked the Goggle with her flyswatter right in his eyes, and Sister Elouise burned the other with her lighter. The Goggles howled and released them.

Sister Elizabeth Thick Glasses wasn't afraid of the mayhem. Because of her lifelong history of poor eyesight—and occasional run-ins with Oyster for using her eyedropper for things other than eye drops—she was used to the blurry speed that was part of the battle. With great confidence, she closed her eyes and seemed to fight with a sixth sense. She anticipated the tongues flying at her, dodged, and chopped them. She moved through the battle like a master.

Sister Hilda Prone to Asthma collected some of the nuns' rosaries and fashioned a lasso. She was wheezing some, yes, but Sister Theresa Raised on a Farm quickly mastered the lasso and the skills of her youth came back to her quickly as she rounded up one Goggle after another, hog-tied them, and threw them into a pile.

Sister Augusta of the Elaborate Belches cornered a few Goggles with her belches alone—like a lioness. And Sister Margaret of the Long Sighs and Withering Glare had Vince Vance backed against the tower's wall with her piercing stare.

The Wingers and the Doggers and prisoners fought hard too. There were bloodshed and cries. Eshma Weegrit was already on her knees tending to some of those lashed by Goggle tongues.

A Goggle tongue snapped out and stuck onto the middle of Leatherbelly's long torso, pulling him in toward a set of sharp Goggle teeth. But Oyster reached out quickly, grabbed Leatherbelly by the collar, and pulled him back as hard as he could, stretching the tongue until it snapped.

In the center of it all, the Goggles protected Dark Mouth with a ringed fortress of flicking tongues. He cried out in anguish, "Where are my vultures? Send in the vultures!"

Quickly, the sky grew dark with the black, beating wings of large birds. The Blood-Beaked Vultures circled overhead, sometimes diving and snapping up Wingers.

The vultures swooped and jabbed Growsels, and as the Doggers got distracted and took aim at the Blood-Beaked Vultures the Goggles attacked more aggressively.

Sister Mary Many Pockets was the first to start flapping at the Blood-Beaked Vultures, but soon the other nuns did, too. They stood tall and bobbed on their toes, clapping their arms over their heads. Their skirts buoyed. Their veils rose and fell.

The vultures were frightened. One vulture who'd begun to dive-bomb a clutch of prisoners got frightened and flew off. Another who was racing toward a delicate Winger stopped midair and began to beat its wings in reverse, then took off for the night sky.

"Yes!" Oyster cheered. "Keep going!"

Quickly, the Blood-Beaked Vultures peeled off and flew away.

The retreating vultures allowed Oyster and his compadres a chance to reattack the Goggles, who were, by and large, pinned to the floor with arrows.

Oyster had an idea. He yelled to Sister Margaret of the Long Sighs and Withering Glare, "I need your cross!"

She pulled it off of her neck and tossed it to him.

Sister Mary Many Pockets was fending off Goggles. "I need your cross and some rope," Oyster called.

Of course she had rope. She had everything in her

many pockets. She tossed him her heavy cross necklace and a long piece of rope. He lassoed the top of the bone-flower that leaned over the metal hook holding his parents, and using the two crosses as a grappling hook, he scaled the flower. He climbed out to the tip of the flower. Here, he saw his parents up close for the first time.

"You're here," Oyster's mother said, her eyes glassy with tears. "After all this time . . . it's really you."

"We've missed you so much," his father said through a sad smile.

Oyster said what he'd wanted to say to someone for a long time now, but, before this adventure, he never could have imagined getting to say it to his very own parents: "I'm here to save you."

Then he shouted to the nuns below, "I need your help!"

Sister Mary Many Pockets knew exactly what he needed. She got the nuns to gather below Oyster's parents and to use their skirts as a net. Oyster's parents watched him as he stretched and reached and stretched some more until he was close enough to use the sword to slice the rope holding them to the hook. His parents dropped quickly and were caught by the net of black skirts, and gently lowered to the ground.

But Oyster wasn't yet finished. Sister Mary Many

Pockets knew his plan. She guided him to just the right High-Tipping Bluebell. As a candle snuffer in the nunnery for years and years, she knew how to help him. Oyster chopped the High-Tipping Bluebell, hacking at it with the sword. Its bell-shaped bloom, now the consistency of bone, fell on the flame of the Torch. It stuck there, stem in the air.

The fire went out.

And a cheer rose up—a cheer from the Wingers, chests aglow; the Doggers, Ippy, and Drusser; Hopps and all of the nuns; the prisoners and Oyster's parents; Leatherbelly yipping joyfully. The cheer poured into the valley and clear across to Boneland on the other side.

The Goggles were weary. Vince Vance, cornered by Sister Margaret of the Long Sighs and Withering Glare, dropped his dagger. Dark Mouth suddenly looked scared. With no one to protect him, the crowd was inching around him menacingly.

"No! No!" he roared.

From his high perch, Oyster had to catch his breath for a moment. He looked out across the valley to Boneland. It looked like a quaint, little winter scene. The snow looked like moths flitting, which made Oyster think of his moth collection. How he loved to keep them in the mesh box and watch them, and pretend that they understood that he was their friend. And in an instant, Oyster thought he might understand Dark Mouth. Maybe he'd wanted the Perths as pets. He'd wanted to pretend that they were his friends without ever really knowing how to talk to them or really be friends with them. He didn't turn the flowers to stony bones to kill them, it struck Oyster now, but . . .

Oyster looked down at Dark Mouth and the tightening knot of the angry crowd. He shouted, "Wait! Wait! Listen. I think I understand him."

Everyone below looked up, even Dark Mouth. Oyster said, "Dark Mouth wanted the Map destroyed because he didn't want anyone to be able to leave him. He wanted everything to stay just as it was when his father was alive." Oyster stared directly at Dark Mouth now. He said, "You didn't hate your father. You loved him. You wanted to keep his flowers just the way he'd left them, forever. You're afraid that if the Map exists, Perths and Doggers and everyone will find a way to leave you. And you don't want to be alone!"

Everyone was stunned by this notion. They blinked their eyes and gawked at Dark Mouth.

"Of course not!" Dark Mouth shouted. "I had my *own* reasons!" Dark Mouth got even angrier and began swinging his large, unwieldy arms at the crowd. As Oyster tried to scramble back down the bone-flower he saw a white clump fly off of Dark Mouth's arm. The crowd ran screaming. Then another bit fell off and another clump broke free and hit Vince Vance in the back. He fell to the ground as if he'd been shot.

Dark Mouth seemed as if he was coming apart. His outside coating was breaking up, and he didn't seem massive and weighty at all. He appeared airy, as if he were nothing more than a big balloon.

Oyster spotted Leatherbelly down below, who was completely ignoring Dark Mouth's antics. He looked tired and hungry. He probably hadn't eaten in ages; he had the exhausted look of a dog who'd been shoved through ductwork and battled Goggles. When a clump landed at Leatherbelly's paws, he sniffed it and then ate it. He looked quite pleased.

The crowd stood still as Dark Mouth bounced and bipped around overhead.

"What's happening?" Vince Vance shouted. "Dark Mouth! Speak to me!"

"He's coming undone," Hopps said.

It was at this moment that Leatherbelly decided to take an enormous bite. He was waddling along Dark Mouth's wobbly base. He sank his teeth into something taut, and there was a loud pop followed by a hiss of air. The large white creature deflated like a balloon. It roiled and listed from side to side. It had spiny, jointed innards that, as the beast deflated, poked through the sugar-coated material, like broken metal bones. Finally it writhed and fell in on itself until there was just a large, flattened, sugar-crusted sack.

"Dark Mouth is gone!" Oyster shouted.

A cheer sprang up. Everyone jumped and shouted for joy. Oyster looked at the nuns, whooping it up, their veils a-billow. He looked at Sister Mary Many Pockets, whose heart was pure bliss, and then at his parents, who beamed at him. But it was all so much, he felt overcome. The unlit wick of the Torch overhead was still smoking. He watched the thin plume rise into the air and disappear.

CHAPTER 23

A BROKEN PORTAL

Of course there was joy and mad *hoot-hoot*ing and loud *rah-rah*ing in the streets of Boneland—a noise as loud and excited as that of fifty Happy Fig Days rolled into one. Doggers, Wingers, Perths, even most of the Goggles—who, as it turned out, didn't particularly care for all of the hostility—danced and *yawp*ed together. And the nuns joined in too, kicking it up as if at a silver jubilee.

Oyster, however, missed it. He was exhausted. When they'd finally gotten back to Ringet's apartment, he collapsed into a deep sleep. He dreamed fitfully—and oddly enough, of only two things: a shop filled with maps and the Mapkeeper with her oxygen tank on wheels. He was in her shop trying to apologize for stealing his map, trying to explain all that had happened. He was trying to tell her that he'd had trouble but that it had worked out okay in the end. She wasn't listening, however. She was busy setting up shop. "I have no time for chatter! So many children, so many Worlds to chart!" And then Oyster looked out of the window, and it wasn't Baltimore. It was Boneland, except that it was no longer polluted with sugar. It looked like spring. The Mapkeeper appeared at his side. "There is more to the story, Oyster. You know only a tiny sliver. More work for a hero to do." The dream kept playing itself out, over and over.

Oyster woke only to eat and then smile at Sister Mary Many Pockets and his parents, who took turns at his bedside. And then he would sleep again. Eshma visited often with specially brewed teas. She said that his weariness was quite normal. He'd regain his strength in a few days.

Sister Mary Many Pockets let his parents have their time. She tried not to hover. She ate peanuts and sat at Ringet's table and tried to mend the Map. From her many pockets, she pulled out glue, tape—duct and Scotch and mailing varieties—plus a needle and thread. Sister Helen Quick Fingers tried to knit it together too.

Nothing worked.

Eshma had given it the once-over. "Broken portal," she said. "It might not heal." She went on to explain that it was hard to say if it was the wild commotion of the thirteen desperate nuns or if it was the violent rupture when they left the Map or if it was the evil presence of Dark Mouth, or a combination. . . . But the fact was this: The Slippery Map was broken.

Hopps and Ringet huddled nearby. They pretended to be sorry about the broken map, but they weren't convincing.

"So sorry you have to stay," Ringet told Oyster.

Hopps was more blunt. "Oyster could just live here with us."

Sister Mary Many Pockets would smile in just such a way that they knew what she meant.

"Sure we'd love to have you visit as often as possible!" Ringet said.

"And yes, yes, we know," Hopps grumbled. "You all need to be back in your own home."

But, of course, it wasn't clear how they would get home, much less back again for a visit, if the Map couldn't be repaired.

Oli and Marge stopped by with their son. Oyster was sleeping, so they left huge bags of assorted figs.

Ippy and Drusser stopped in too.

Drusser didn't want to get too close, afraid he might wake him. "I knew from the first time I met him that he would save us all," he whispered.

Ippy usually lingered. She liked to spend time with

Oyster's parents. They liked to tell stories about the good old days. Ippy listened and asked questions; sometimes the questions were political, but other times she just wanted to know what her mother liked to wear, what her father liked to sing when he was happy. And Oyster's parents would do a little duet. Sometimes Ippy talked to Oyster, heart-to-heart. *I miss you, Oyster. Wake up soon. Get better quickly.*

When Oyster did finally wake up, fully wide-eyed one night, he said, "Sing that song again, the one about the moon and the girl you love so much."

His parents were there, Sister Mary Many Pockets, Hopps, and Ringet too. Ippy had fallen asleep at the foot of the bed. She was snoring lightly. Eshma was preparing a roots potion to cure Ringet's lock leg. The apartment smelled of dirt and mint.

"Oyster," Hopps said. "You're up!"

Ippy startled awake. "Oyster? You're awake?"

"Ippy!" Oyster said. "You missed me?"

She smiled and nodded. "Like a hole in the head," she said.

"I'll make some tea!" Ringet said, calling to Eshma. "He's up! He's up!"

Oyster's mother said, "Hello, Oyster."

Oyster's father said, "Listen. Do you hear them outside, rejoicing? It's for you. Thank you for saving all of us." They were sitting on the edge of the bed. His mother was holding his hand. Hers felt soft and warm. Sister Mary Many Pockets was standing near the door, as if she was unsure whether to stay or go.

Her heart spoke softly. It said, *This might be private. It might not include me.*

"You know Hopps and Ringet and Ippy, here," Oyster said to his parents, "but do you know Sister Mary Many Pockets?"

They all nodded.

"You've been asleep for days, Oyster," Hopps explained.

"Have I?"

"Yes," Hopps said.

"We're all okay now," Oyster's mother said. She cupped his face in her hand.

Oyster couldn't help himself. He leaned into it. "I'm so happy here," he said.

And Sister Mary Many Pockets nodded. She understood. She took a small step backward.

"But I want to go home, too," Oyster said. "I miss home."

Oyster's mother smiled. "Of course, Oyster," she said. "We wouldn't keep you from your home."

"Can you have two homes?" his father asked.

"Can you have three?" Hopps added.

Sister Mary Many Pockets was all choked up. Her face blushed sweetly. She crossed her arms and shook her head. *Oyster R. Motel,* her heart was saying, *I love you so.*

The nuns were back from the celebrations. They were humming and swaying, their faces pink and exhausted. When they saw that Oyster was awake, they rushed him with hugs. Some wept, others laughed. Some did both at the same time.

Sister Mary Many Pockets hadn't yet explained to the nuns that the Map was truly broken. She didn't want to alarm them. But now that Oyster was up, they assumed that it was time to leave. They scribbled good-byes to Hopps and Ringet, Oyster's parents and Ippy. They scribbled, *Thank you for your gracious hosting.*

Sister Mary Many Pockets held up her hands, wrote her note, and handed it to Oyster to read. He needed to know too.

Oyster read, *The Slippery Map is broken. I can't fix it.* He looked at Eshma Weegrit.

She shrugged. "It's true! Nothing I can do either."

He stopped there and looked up at Sister Mary Many Pockets. "Are you sure?"

Sister Mary Many Pockets nodded yes.

The nuns harumphed and coughed and generally fidgeted.

"If only we had another map," Eshma said. "If only . . ."

And that's when Oyster thought of it. He snapped his fingers. "Ringet," he said. "I have a Map of my own!"

Ringet winced, obviously remembering Oyster's sad little Map.

Hopps shook his head. "Oyster, c'mon now. I don't really think—"

"Get it out of the soup can!" Oyster said. "I've been imagining! I really have! I have let my imagination loose."

Ringet walked to the shelf and pulled on the oversized soup can. It had surprising weight, and Ringet caught it awkwardly in his skinny arms. "My, my," he said, passing the can to Oyster.

Oyster looked inside. His Map was full and fat. It filled the oversized soup can so tightly that it was hard to

wedge it out. But he finally did. He rolled it on the bed and there it was: the house he'd imagined with his parents, the backyard with the swing set, the garden, the clothesline. On one side of the Map there was the Gulf of Wind and Darkness, which led to Boneland and what was now called the Breathing River of Nunly Snores. There was a large section on the underground field with all of the eye and fire holes of Dragons marked clearly Evil Fishback Field—and the Dragons were red. Dark Mouth's prison, the Torch, drawn with exact detail, including the shiny silver hook. On the other side, Oyster saw the nunnery and the Dragon Palace and the chair where the boy with leg braces sat and the library of Johns Hopkins and Dr. Fromler's Dentistry and, not far off, the Mapkeeper's shop.

"It's all here!" Oyster said. "Look at all of the details!" He looked at the Mapkeeper's shop again. It reminded him of his dream. He sat up on his knees and looked out of Ringet's window. Outside, the sugar-snow was gone, and it looked like spring, just like in his dream. Blue Iglits, no longer confined to hidden indoor locations like Ringet's apartment, now darted through the air. Oyster glanced back at his Map. He found Ringet's apartment and put a finger on it.

"What is it?" Hopps asked.

He drew a line across the street and found, on the

other side, another version of the Mapkeeper's shop. Oyster looked out the window again, and there it was. A shop—no sign on the door except one that read: GOING OUT OF BUSINESS. He saw a figure move past the glass front of the shop and then to the front door. There she was—locking up with a key, rolling her oxygen tank. Oyster waved.

"Who is it?" Oyster's parents asked.

"Someone you know too, I think," Oyster said.

But the Mapkeeper kept on strolling, and by the time Oyster's parents looked across the street, she was gone.

"Who?" his father asked.

"I don't see anyone," his mother said.

Oyster slid down. The Mapkeeper knew more than she'd let on. She was a player in all of this. Oyster wasn't sure how. There was a story here and he would want to know it, all of it. Now that his parents were here, there would be time to hear as much as they had to tell.

"Never mind," he said. "There's time for that later." He pointed to the Map. "This is a house for you," he said to his parents. "It's halfway between the nunnery and here. See it? There's a garden and a swing set. And I can spend some of my time there with you, like a regular family. Ippy can come and play there with me. Ringet and Hopps can come for dinner."

His parents nodded.

"We'd like that," his mother said.

"Very much," his father added.

"And then I can come here sometimes." He pointed to Ringet's apartment.

"Yes, yes!" Ringet and Hopps said happily. "Rah-rah and hoot-hoot!"

"And here's the nunnery, where I'll stay with Sister Mary Many Pockets and the nuns," he said, and then he paused and looked at them. "I'm not listless and dull. I'm not even nunlike. I'm just a regular boy. But, well, is that okay with you all?" he asked.

The nuns all smiled and nodded vigorously, especially Sister Mary Many Pockets, whose heart cheered, *It was always okay for you to be yourself!*

"And right now that's where I'd like to be: in my own bed in the nunnery surrounded by snores."

Everyone agreed that the plan sounded just right.

"We have a responsibility to put things in order here," his father said. "Then we'll come to visit you in the house you imagined for us, the one with the swing set, the garden, and the clothesline."

"It won't take long. We'll visit soon! We love you so!"

Oyster nodded. "You're the ones who started all of this," he said. "I guess you should make sure it's all set right."

The good-byes were sad and cheery, both. They'd all

found one another. That was worth celebrating, and now that they had Oyster's Map to pass through, they would see one another again soon. They hugged each other for a good long time.

Hopps and Ringet put their fingers to the sides of their noses. Oyster returned the gesture.

Oyster used the bucket charm on his necklace to open his Map right to the convent's broom closet. Ringet's apartment filled with breezes. The nuns stepped into the Map, one by one, and disappeared. Oyster was second to last. He waved wildly.

They all waved back, quite teary-eyed: Eshma, Ippy, his mother and father, Ringet, and Hopps. Oyster stepped into the hole, a rush of wind lifted his hair, and he was gone.

This left only Sister Mary Many Pockets.

Oyster's mother said, "You can step into the Map and hold on to its poles at the same time."

His father went on, "Therefore bringing the Map with you through the Gulf of Wind and Darkness so you'll have it on the other side."

She nodded. Yes, yes, she understood.

And then Oyster's parents both hugged her. They whispered, "Thank you. Thank you. Thank you."

But Sister Mary Many Pockets only smiled and shook her head. *Thank you,* she mouthed. *Thank you.*

And then Sister Mary Many Pockets stepped into the Map while gripping its poles. Her skirt billowed. Her veil flew up. She gave a bow and then, with a nearly electric snap, the nun and the Map were gone.

EPILOGUE

Dear Reader,

Well, there you have it. Odd, I know. Odd but true.

The nun who told me this story in the middle of a snowy night in Baltimore was Sister Mary Many Pockets—but, of course, you've guessed that by now. (I forget sometimes how perceptive you are.)

She wrote down this story for me on slips of paper, but not in these words. She gave me a summary of the story, and I held on to those little slips of paper for dear life.

When she finished and we were sitting quietly in the nunnery kitchen, I thought, *Bode*—for that's what I call myself when I'm giving myself the straight-talk—*you might very well have a great book on these little scraps of paper. You might just prove to all those other writers that you are not a fraud!*

Sister Mary Many Pockets called a cab for me, and while we waited she decided that she still had one thing to show me. She ushered me up the nunnery stairs to the hall of bedrooms. It was as noisy as the Breathing River, certainly. She turned into Oyster's room. It was different from how she'd described it earlier. It now had bunk beds. Oyster, however, was sleeping in a sleeping bag on the floor. He was a little sweaty in his heavy blankets, but rosy. And a small girl—a miniature version of a girl, a young Perth, in fact, with an impish face and freckles—was sleeping on the bottom bunk. It was Ippy, of course. And on the top bunk was a boy with black hair: the owner's son from the Dragon Palace. And since there were no leg braces or crutches, and since he was on the top bunk, I have to assume that Eshma cured him.

At the foot of Oyster's sleeping bag was a slim dachs-hund stretched out in all of his glory. I suppose he refused to go back to Mrs. Fishback—maybe he even gave her one of the growls she'd taught him long before.

Sister Mary Many Pockets handed me a note that said, *A sleepover. Best friends.*

She then led me back to the main door. The cab was waiting at the curb. I said, "Thank you for the notes." I was still holding them tightly to my chest.

She looked at me and tilted her head, and that's when I heard her say something to me. It went some-thing like: *Will you write this story down?*

I nodded. "Yes, yes," I said. "I promise."

And then her heart—what else could it have been?—said, *You don't need those notes, N. E. Bode. You have the story lodged within you. It's yours now to tell.*

I nodded, a little surprised and shaken. I thanked her again and shuffled off the stoop. I walked to the cab, but before I opened the door, I looked back at Sister Mary Many Pockets. Her chubby hands folded together at her chest as if at that very moment she was saying a prayer for me, Bode with his bundle of notes.

I took her in. I really did. And then I threw both arms up into the air, and the notes drifted out and up like more snow, like sugar, like moths.

And so here I am. N. E. Bode, Author.

I hand this story to you with reverence and diligence and a fat imagination and love,

NE Bode

N. E. Bode